the

vampire

is just

not

that

into

you

vlad mezrich

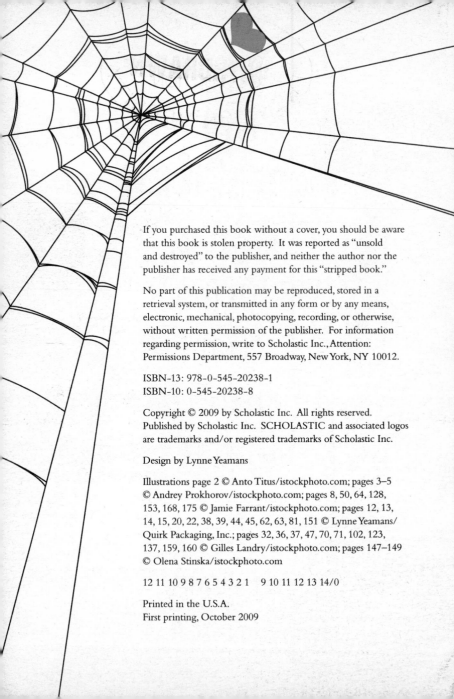

ISBN-13: 978-0-545-20238-1
ISBN-10: 0-545-20238-8

Design by Lynne Yeamans

Illustrations page 2 © Anto Titus/istockphoto.com; pages 3–5 © Andrey Prokhorov/istockphoto.com; pages 8, 50, 64, 128, 153, 168, 175 © Jamie Farrant/istockphoto.com; pages 12, 13, 14, 15, 20, 22, 38, 39, 44, 45, 62, 63, 81, 151 © Lynne Yeamans/ Quirk Packaging, Inc.; pages 32, 36, 37, 47, 70, 71, 102, 123, 137, 159, 160 © Gilles Landry/istockphoto.com; pages 147–149 © Olena Stinska/istockphoto.com

12 11 10 9 8 7 6 5 4 3 2 1   9 10 11 12 13 14/0

Printed in the U.S.A.
First printing, October 2009

the author
would like to thank

David Levithan
Erin Black
Rachel Griffiths
Mallory Kass
Victoria Kosara
J. R. Mortimer
Jennifer Rees
Gregory Rutty
and Divya Sawhney
*for their contributions
to this book.*

*Truly, I feel that
each of you is
a part of me.*

contents

So . . .
you want
to date a
vampire.

this is not a question. Of course you want to date a vampire. Who doesn't want to date a vampire?

You might think it's as easy as showing a little neck, picking a few scabs, and looking helpless in all the right places (when a car's about to hit you, when a mountain lion's about to eat you, when the teacher calls on you and you don't know the answer because you've been daydreaming about your hypothetical vampire lover, etc.). But it's not as simple as that. Sure, sometimes you might be able to warm the space where his heart used to be. But a lot of the time, the vampire is just not that into you.

You'd think that vampires would be easy to read, with their astonishingly translucent skin and all. Well, think again. Telling the difference can be a matter of life and death for your relationship (as well as a matter of life and death for your, well, life).

This book is meant to help. I, Vlad Mezrich, will show you all the ins and outs, ups and downs, bleedings and healings of dating a vampire. I will let you know what he's thinking when he's with you, what he's thinking when he's without you, and what you can do to make him yours—morning, noon, and twilight.

After all, it takes one to know one. And I, Vlad Mezrich, most definitely am one.

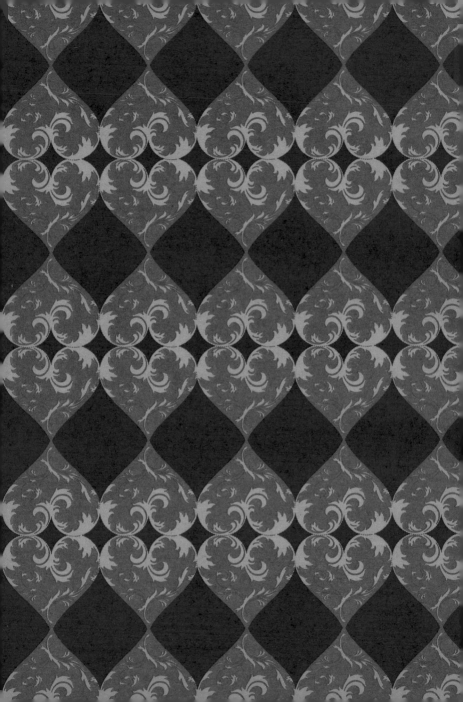

❧

your crush has bite

is he a vampire, or just a vampire wannabe?

Many girls have said to me, "Vlad, sometimes it's so hard to find the right vampire. I go after all the wrong ones. Some of them even turn out to be . . . human!"

Believe me, I understand this confusion. It used to be so easy to tell everyone apart. The difference between a vampire and a human was as clear as the difference between drinking blood and drinking Pepsi. But then the wannabes appeared—human boys who dress themselves up like vampires in order to get girls. They'll say they're doing it for other reasons (they like a certain band; they think they look good in black; they're anemic), but, trust me, they're only trying to trap girls into loving them. *Do not fall for this.* You deserve much more than a knockoff. You deserve the real undead.

I am *never* dating a human guy again. You know what they say, "Once you go vamp, you never decamp." First of all, vampires are *hot*. And not in that "if I squint you kinda look like Chace Crawford if his face was swollen from an allergic reaction" sort of way. I mean *really* hot. They don't get acne. They have amazing bodies because blood is really low in carbs. Even their facial expressions are sexy! Vampires spend most of their time sneering. You can never tell if a vampire is scoffing at your outfit, or debating between killing you and asking you out! (I *love* to be kept guessing. It keeps things interesting.)

— EMMA, 17

The first way to figure out whether or not the guy you're interested in is a true vampire is to consider his physical appearance. In this case, you *can* judge a book by its cover—and find out whether the book is a sexy, throbbing, poetic story of eternal devotion or a wussy, lame, inarticulate pamphlet of human inadequacy.

checking him out: undead

✛
vampire

Eye color ranging from tawny gold to jet-black, and occasionally crimson. Crafty vampires will sometimes wear colored contacts, but there's a surefire way to tell if he's *truly* undead. Does his expression say he wants to devour you? Congratulations! You've got a 100% Grade A vampire on your hands!

Hair is perfectly tousled. No, it's perfect! No, it's tousled!

Breath is magically minty.

Look for a curved white fang. Elongated incisors are a dead giveaway, but blinding white teeth that gleam in the dark also indicate supernatural status.

Find an excuse to lean your head against his perfectly chiseled chest. No heartbeat? Kudos!

Skin is brilliant white and firm as marble. Extra points if he sparkles!

Indescribably delicious smell. It's like ~~sun after a rainstorm, longing, ice melting in fire that's somehow freezing again, cookies?~~ Sorry, it's actually indescribable.

...or dud
✤
human

Annoying lack of supersonic hearing. Says "huh?" sometimes when you whisper secrets to him.

Smile is only semi-crooked.

Pasty pale skin . . . but prone to breakouts.

Bleeds.

Can't even fly.

He's the captain of the football team and the basketball team, and he can run a five-minute mile. But who cares? If he can't jump up to your second-story window, he's not undead enough for you.

Has a strong, sweet scent . . . that's suspiciously similar to Abercrombie Fierce.

✠ decoding his online profile ✠

I can hear you now: *But, Vlad, you're assuming that I always have in-person interactions with my crush! That's so twentieth century!* Now, there's no reason to be rude—I have profiles on at least twelve different social networking sites. I've found so many of my old friends that way—vampires I hadn't seen in hundreds of years! After you've located a potential vampire, it's time to examine his online profile for clues.

✠ example a

Name: Will Barnes

Status: Will is stoked by the surf report. Swell's coming in! (updated 10:43 a.m.)

Interests: Baseball, working out, chillin' with my friends, generally being awesome

Favorite Books: *The Great Gatsby, 1000 Ways to Cook Beef*

Favorite Music: Fall Out Boy, The Killers, basically anything that gets me pumped

Quotes: "Dude, that's sick." —me, like every time Doug talks

Not promising. Vampires don't spend much time at the beach or wake up early to update their profiles.

Excellent! Vampires love baseball.

Vampires avoid the gym as it's difficult to look brooding and tortured on an elliptical machine.

Bad sign. Vampires don't need to tell people they're awesome—they just ARE.

Human guys often list this book because it's assigned in class. A good test is to ask the guy what happens at the end. If he knows, vampire! If not, human. :-(

Not so promising, but could be a clever ruse! Vampires are slick like that.

Vampires hate getting pumped.

Vampire meter: LOW

✴ example b

Name: (Quentin Davenport)

Old-fashioned name! Means he could've been born in another century.

Status: Quentin is thirsty.
(updated 3:12 a.m.)

Interests: (Classical music,) the way moonlight reflects off a frozen mountain lake at 3 a.m., baseball

Don't worry if your vampire candidate sounds a bit . . . melancholy. Most vampires are super angsty. It's just their thing. Go with it.

Favorite Books: (War and Peace,) (Being and Nothingness,) (How to Speak Like You Were Born in the Twentieth Century)

Vampires love long books 'cause they have a lot of time to kill.

They also have time to think really deep thoughts.

Sweet!

Favorite Music: Debussy, Mendelssohn, the sound of blood pumping through the left ventricle

Quotes: "When old age shall this generation waste/ Thou shalt (remain,) in the midst of other woe"
 —Keats, "Ode on a Grecian Urn"

Awesome! Vampires LOVE to complain about being hot and immortal.

Vampire meter: SUPER HIGH

When I was dating Ben, this human guy, he spent every Friday night with his friends playing Halo and misquoting lines from *The 40-Year-Old Virgin*. Now I go over to my vampire boyfriend's house and he plays songs he writes for me on the piano. Last week, Nathaniel wrote the most beautiful piece inspired by the sight of me flossing. I didn't even know that he sat in the tree outside my bathroom every night! It's so romantic.

—DANIELLE, 16

Before I met my vampire, Alaric, I was just the clumsy new girl with low self-esteem. But since we've started dating, suddenly everyone wants me. It's not just the A/V guys or the student council dorks, it's also the jocks, the preps, the trackers, and a whole pack of local werewolves! At this point, I don't even *care* if Alaric is just after my blood. At least I'll die popular!

—MANDY, 15

dealing with posers

I recognize that sometimes posers will slip through—they are so devoted to their subcultures that their human tendencies slip past normal filters. Three groups tend to give girls the hardest problems when determining whether or not a boy is a vampire:

POSER TYPE A ✣ goth

They take posing to the highest level, although they tend to accessorize much, much more than a vampire ever would. **Their devotion is admirable, but their humanity is not.** 💧💧💧

POSER TYPE B ✣ emo

We had a phrase for these boys in the sixteenth century, and that was *drama queens.* Big distinction: Vampires know that they're going to live forever, while emo boys act like they're going to die forever. **Which one would you rather spend your time with?** 💧💧

POSER TYPE AB ✣ gamer

In fairness, this group holds no vampiric aspiration. It's just that they get no sleep, have horribly bloodshot eyes, and mainly stay indoors, out of the sun. **As a result, they are often confused for vampires, in the rare moments when they peel themselves away from the PlayStation, Xbox, or Wii.** 💧

💧💧💧 **= major poser** 💧💧 **= poser wannabe** 💧 **= no pose whatsoever**

is he a goth, emo, gamer, or vampire?

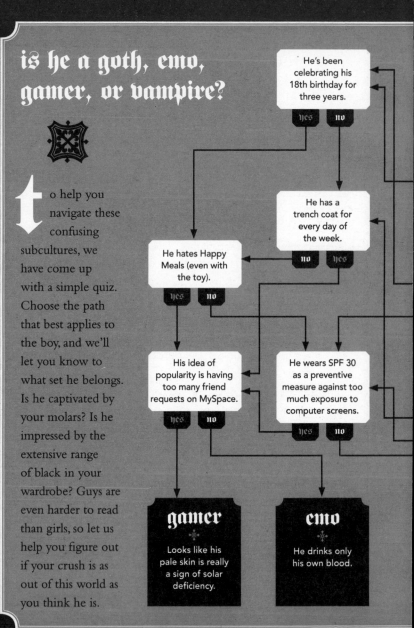

o help you navigate these confusing subcultures, we have come up with a simple quiz. Choose the path that best applies to the boy, and we'll let you know to what set he belongs. Is he captivated by your molars? Is he impressed by the extensive range of black in your wardrobe? Guys are even harder to read than girls, so let us help you figure out if your crush is as out of this world as you think he is.

He's been celebrating his 18th birthday for three years.

yes   no

He has a trench coat for every day of the week.

no   yes

He hates Happy Meals (even with the toy).

yes   no

His idea of popularity is having too many friend requests on MySpace.

yes   no

He wears SPF 30 as a preventive measure against too much exposure to computer screens.

yes   no

gamer

Looks like his pale skin is really a sign of solar deficiency.

emo

He drinks only his own blood.

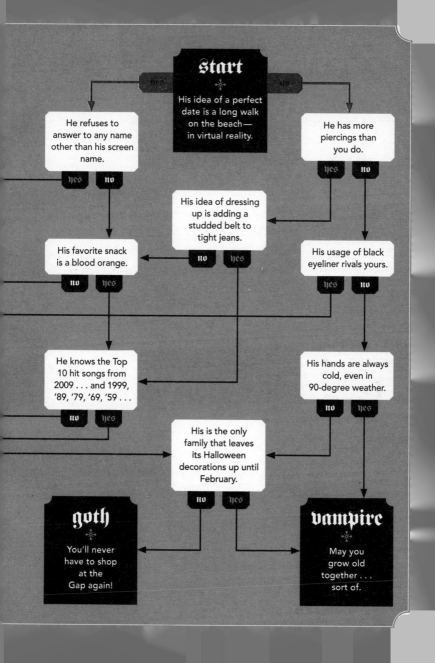

Finally, there are distinct verbal clues that can tell you whether the boy you like is a vampire or just plays one in his own mind.

WHAT A human SAYS: "Nice dress!"
WHAT A vampire SAYS: "That dress is almost as glorious a creation as you, my beloved. It makes me want to dance endlessly through time with you."

WHAT A human SAYS: "I don't know — what do you want to do?"
WHAT A vampire SAYS: "Wherever you go, I will follow. Whatever you want to experience, I will cling lovingly to you as you experience it."

WHAT A human SAYS: "I'm hungry."
WHAT A vampire SAYS: "I want you."

WHAT A human SAYS: "You're such a tease."
WHAT A vampire SAYS: "The fact that we can never be together only emboldens my desire. To touch you . . . a hope. To kiss you . . . a dream."

Once you've figured out that the object of your affection is a vampire (and of course he is!), then you must decide whether he is the right vampire for you.

But, Vlad, you're protesting, *all I want is a vampire! They're all such paragons of virile, aloof, passionate, undead manliness. Any vampire will do, right?*

Wrong! While human guys are, for the most part, completely interchangeable, vampire males are most certainly not!

types of human and vampire males

HUMAN MALES

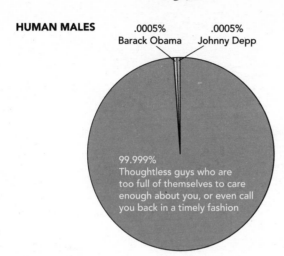

.0005%
Barack Obama

.0005%
Johnny Depp

99.999%
Thoughtless guys who are too full of themselves to care enough about you, or even call you back in a timely fashion

VAMPIRE MALES

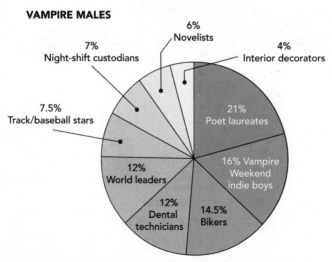

6%
Novelists

7%
Night-shift custodians

4%
Interior decorators

7.5%
Track/baseball stars

21%
Poet laureates

16% Vampire
Weekend
indie boys

12%
World leaders

12%
Dental
technicians

14.5%
Bikers

finding the vampire who's right for you

Like snowflakes falling on a newly unearthed casket, every vampire is unique, and the key to a successful relationship (at least at first) is to find the snowflake that fits best on your tongue. Don't just settle for the nearest available vampire — find the vampire who's right for *you*.

Our quiz reveals the prince of darkness who will light up *your* night!

1. **You'll swoon on the first date if he:**
   a. Saves you from being crushed by a truck, *then* thwarts your would-be murderers in a dark alley.
   b. Abducts you from a Transylvanian town.
   c. Skips the preliminaries and goes straight for your heart.

2. **What's his signature style?**
   a. You think he's an Abercrombie guy . . . but honestly, you're usually too busy staring at the glory of his face to notice what he's wearing.
   b. Mostly capes and tight-fitting suits. On special occasions, he shows up as a bat.
   c. Your feral mountain man is too rugged to think about clothes. He barely remembers to wear shoes!

3. Your preferred pet name is:

a. My Unbearably Fragile Human Love. Leave me! No, stay!

b. *Fleur d'Morte.*

c. Lunch.

4. Things are getting kind of steamy. He kisses you passionately and:

a. Pushes you away in a burst of superhuman self-restraint. The smell of your blood is just too intoxicating!

b. Runs his fangs along your neck. Fingers crossed—it might be time for you to become his latest vampire bride!

c. Rips your throat out. It's okay, though. You've always wanted to die for love.

5. His preferred mode of travel is:

a. In exotic foreign cars, preferably expensive.

b. By bat.

c. Running through the woods really, really fast.

6. Five senses just won't hack it. Your ideal undead also has:

a. Mind-reading skills.

b. The ability to fly.

c. An uncanny way of always knowing *exactly* where you are.

7. His future plans for you include:

a. You getting wrinkly while he remains your hot young thing.

b. It's eternity! You're joining him in unholy marriage . . . along with his twelve other undead brides.

c. Strangely, he keeps saying you don't have a future.

⇤ Scoring ⇥

IF YOU ANSWERED MOSTLY A's

You have an Edward on your hands! He'll raise your pulse, but his emo ways will also make your head spin. He'll push you away, but his yearning eyes will pull you back again. He'll leave you for your own good, and then come back the second you start to get over him. It's exhausting, but . . . you know you love it.

IF YOU ANSWERED MOSTLY B's

The bachelor behind coffin B is: Vlad the Impaler! Putting the "prince" in "prince of darkness," Vlad the Impaler–types tend to be descended from Transylvanian nobility. They're proud of their heritage, so everything about them is old-school—from their silk-lined coffins to their silk-lined capes. Play hard to get if you want *this* vampire. Try wearing a flimsy robe on the nearest moonlit balcony—he'll eat you up!

IF YOU ANSWERED MOSTLY C's

Admit it: You're drawn to bad boys, like James. A James–type is rough and ready, the kind of guy who would ride a motorcycle . . . if he couldn't already outrun it. He isn't that charming and he isn't that hot, but he'll track you to the ends of the earth if you catch his interest. Just make sure you play it cool—this guy will rip out your heart . . . if you let him!

the ten best places to meet a vampire

Check out these vampire hot spots to find the undead of your dreams. Of course, if none of these locations work for you, you can also (as the tales say) have a virgin boy ride naked and saddle-less on a virgin stallion through a graveyard until the horse steps on a grave and goes no farther. But of course, that raises the question: Where are you going to find a horse?

1 ✤ the blood bank

You're there to give, and he's there to take. You may feel a little woozy when the nurse draws your blood, but that's *nothing* compared to what he'll be feeling. You'll get a cookie afterward to keep your blood sugar up, but you won't need it—he'll already be totally sweet on you.

2 ✤ church

Not during services—you didn't think your vampire was a regular churchgoer, did you? No, you have to come back late at night. Very late at night. When no one else is around. And moonlight is streaming in through the stained-glass windows. And candles are flickering in the wind. Vampires can't resist this setup. Just make sure to keep the cross on the wall and not held up in his face.

3 ✣ the school cafeteria

Since vampires tend to cluster at lunchtime, the cafeteria is one of the best spots in school to spot them. Pretty good tip-offs that a clique is undead? They're not eating much. They stare broodingly at one another. When someone who isn't a vampire tries to sit at their table, they hiss. And, of course, they always look tired and sit away from the windows.

---

4 ✣ home depot

It's open all night and has all the things you need to make a comfy casket. At 4:00 in the morning, there's not much to watch on TV, so vampires love to hang out here. Just don't confuse them with the guys who have to work the midnight-to-8 a.m. shift, 'cause they tend to look like they're undead, too.

---

5 ✣ gym class

That hot guy wearing shorts? Not a vampire. That hot guy wearing all black from head to toe and hitting the badminton birdie so hard that it leaves a mark on the floor? Probably a vampire. If you want to get his attention, faint. If you *really* want to get his attention, skin your knee when you dive for the birdie.

---

6 ✣ the forest

The moonlight flickering through the wind-blown branches will give your skin a pale glow. Look a little lost and a little forlorn, and he'll be there faster than you can say "vampire bait."

7 ✳ a parapet

Ideally, the parapet should be stone, decorated with gargoyles, and drenched in shadow. Visiting from 11 p.m. to 3 a.m. on nights with a full moon is highly recommended. Unfortunately, too few modern towns have parapets, but balconies, water towers, and even fire escapes will do in a pinch.

---

8 ✳ graveyards

It may sound obvious, but graveyards are great places to get abducted. Wend your way, sighing, through the crypts, or stray off the paths into the darker sections and see if you don't rustle up a little Saturday-night action. Tip: Wear a long, trailing skirt, and be sure to trip over it as you "run away." Vampires love it when you flirt!

---

9 ✳ caves

If you step into a cave and hear the Cure playing, odds are you're about to hit a vampire's lair. Remember: You might see dark shadows everywhere—but it's probably just his black clothes hanging up to dry. Proceed with excited caution.

---

10 ✳ bookstores

If you're reading this in a bookstore right now (instead of purchasing it—shame on you!), there very well might be a vampire right around the corner. They can often be found shelving books like *Dracula* and *Twilight* in the Biography section instead of Fiction.

I met Max late at night at a twenty-four-hour Walgreens. He was in Aisle 4: Dental Hygiene. I was picking up my Crest Whitestrips when I saw him flossing his teeth right in the aisle! He noticed me staring at his fangs so he came up and said, "How *you* doin'?" If he wasn't so cute I would have given him a look and walked out . . . but I'm totally into a guy with clean teeth.

—MEGAN, 16

inding the right vampire is not the same thing as making him yours. (Or having him decide to make you his.) In chapter three, we will discuss how to make your move. But before we do that, there's another part of the equation we need to consider: you.

A NOTE FROM GRETA, A VAMPIRE SLAYER

Don't get me wrong. I know why you're into him. One minute you're chasing after your tall, pale, and undeniably handsome vampire in a dark alley, stake in hand, ready to do your job as the slayer — and the next, you're ending a date by racing to get inside by 5:30 A.M. to avoid the sunrise that could make him burst into flames. Yeah, it's all such a rush in the beginning.

But then the honeymoon stage is over and you have to decide between going on a romantic nocturnal picnic at the cemetery or doing your job (and potentially wiping out half his extended family). It's hard enough trying to save the world without worrying whether you accidentally killed your vampire boyfriend's uncle Al. Too much stress, girlfriends. Are you really that into him?

are you his (blood) type?

your mother may have told you that vampires are after one thing and one thing only: blood. But that is, at best, a gross oversimplification—if not an outright slander. Vampires are complex beings with complex desires. If we went after every girl who came along, there would be far fewer single vampires—and even fewer living girls.

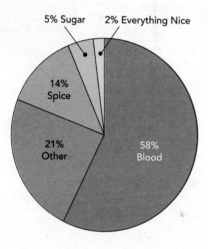

5% Sugar   2% Everything Nice

14% Spice

21% Other

58% Blood

While I personally find the phrase *vampire bait* to be demeaning, there is truth in the impulse to make yourself presentable for a vampire suitor. And by "presentable," I don't mean dressing in black and pricking your finger. I've asked a few of my more attractive vampire friends to weigh in on the age-old question: *What do you look for in a girl?*, and you'll find their responses throughout this chapter. I'll also give you the necessary information you need to draw a vampire to you like a moth to a flame—only without that whole self-immolation part. (It means *burning yourself up*, girls. *Burning yourself up!*)

I go for a nice smile, a great personality, and
0-negative blood.

—SIMON, 902

+—◄◆►—+

I like a girl who doesn't, like, ask me to turn
her into a vampire on the first date. I mean, whoa,
what's the rush? I want to get to know you first!

—THEO, 112

+—◄◆►—+

I love it when a girl seems pretty smart, but then
she manages to put her life in danger at least
twice a day, so she's utterly dependent on me to
rescue her. If she's pretty, I'll totally save her
every time.

—JOSEPH, 73

are you really the kind of girl he wants to sink his fangs into?

His caliginous clothing gives you goose bumps, his alabaster skin is irresistible, but how do you know if you make him want to take flight or stay up with you all night? Take our quiz to find out.

1. **On a sunny summer day, you are probably:**
   a. At the beach, slathering on tanning oil.
   b. Moping around an indie record store.
   c. Sleeping until sundown with the shades drawn.

2. **What dish would you cook for a romantic dinner?**
   a. Steak tartare.
   b. Linguine with garlic and olive oil.
   c. Vegan grilled-cheese sandwiches.

3. **If he sends you flowers, you'll be really happy if the bouquet is mostly:**
   a. Wolfsbane.
   b. Dried moonflowers.
   c. Flowers are so common. How about a branch from a weeping willow?

4. **What time of day are you the most active?**
   a. "Active" isn't really my thing.
   b. At sunrise. The first light really gets me going.
   c. Right around midnight.

5. When you see blood, you:
a. Don't care. Whatever — it's just blood. We're all going to die.
b. Get an adrenaline rush and faint.
c. Vomit.

6. If he looked through your closet, he would mostly find:
a. Polo shirts in every pastel color that exists.
b. Skinny jeans.
c. Vintage eighteenth-century corsets.

7. Your ideal guy is best at what sport?
a. Tossing stones at peasants from his castle window.
b. Soccer.
c. Skateboarding.

8. Your biggest fear is:
a. Being misunderstood.
b. The dark.
c. A tanning bed.

9. If you were walking by a cemetery at night, you'd probably:
a. Stop in for a bit. It would feel like home.
b. Walk quickly and hold your breath for as long as possible.
c. Write a song about the beautiful sorrow of death.

10. Your dream vacation would be:
a. Sailing in the Bahamas.
b. Sipping fair-trade coffee in Williamsburg, Brooklyn.
c. Spelunking in Romanian caves.

╼═ scoring ═╾

GIVE YOURSELF THE FOLLOWING POINTS FOR EACH ANSWER:

1. **a.** 1 **b.** 2 **c.** 3   **2.** **a.** 3 **b.** 2 **c.** 1   **3.** **a.** 1 **b.** 3 **c.** 2

4. **a.** 2 **b.** 1 **c.** 3   **5.** **a.** 2 **b.** 3 **c.** 1   **6.** **a.** 1 **b.** 2 **c.** 3

7. **a.** 3 **b.** 2 **c.** 1   **8.** **a.** 2 **b.** 1 **c.** 3   **9.** **a.** 3 **b.** 1 **c.** 2

10. **a.** 1 **b.** 2 **c.** 3

❄ **FOR A SCORE OF 10 TO 16**

You are not his cup of hemoglobin. You might think he's hot, but this relationship doesn't stand a chance. You're better off with a human boy. You just don't have enough in common to make this work for several lifetimes.

❄ **FOR A SCORE OF 17 TO 23**

You'll have better luck with the emo boy. He may have striking similarities to a vampire, but he's *not* undead—he's moody. Vampires may be attracted to delicate damsels like you, but you don't have what it takes to hold their interest for very long.

❄ **FOR A SCORE OF 24 TO 30**

You really get his blood pumping! (Okay, not in the literal sense, but you know what I mean.) You're like a fragile, red velvet cupcake that he can't wait to nibble on. An eternity of moonlit walks through the graveyard could be in your future.

t's important to remember that no matter how fragile, sweet, pretty, and twisted you are (or aren't), your vampire crush isn't going to be into you unless you have one really big thing going for you: your blood. I know what you're thinking: *But wait, Vlad, just a few pages ago you said that vampires like much more about a girl than just her blood.* True. But we can't ignore blood as an important factor in a vampire's decision-making process. There's a reason he wants to be with you and not, say, a tree.

Think about it this way: Everybody has preferences. Some human guys only date blondes. Others may like piercings or oboe players. Vampires have preferences, too, especially when it comes to blood type. Before you go after your vampire, it's important to know whether you're his type. Remember, you don't have to let him *taste* your blood; the scent alone can be enough to drive him crazy. And it's important to keep him wanting more.

Girls with blue-black hair are especially alluring, because when you play with their hair, you can imagine it's made of veins.

—GUSTAV, 430

I want a girl who will laugh at my jokes even when she's been hearing me tell them for six hundred years.

—IGNATIO, 803

I'm into a girl who doesn't leave the lid up after she goes to the casket.

—GLEN, 194

I'm into pretty girls with long brown hair who love to brood alone for hours at a time in the middle of a forest—that is SO HOT. I mean, they're so quiet, they're practically deer.

—WOLFGANG, AGE 102

I'm looking for confidence! So many girls are so insecure that they look in mirrors all the time. Seriously, I don't mind that I can't see my reflection at all, so why do I want a girl who looks at hers 24/7?

—BARTHOLOMEW, AGE 173

blood type taste test

blood type

TASTE: Full-bodied, woody flavor with notes of cinnamon.

ATTRACTS: Active, clean-cut vampires who enjoy hiking (on cloudy days, of course).

WHERE YOU'LL FIND HIM: Look for the pale guy in the Patagonia fleece—he'll be all over you.

---

blood type

TASTE: Delicate and lingering with notes of vanilla and jasmine. High glucose levels really bring out the flavor, so be sure to nibble on some chocolate beforehand.

ATTRACTS: Introspective, artistic vampires.

WHERE YOU'LL FIND HIM: Staring at you intensely in art class, captivated by your soulful eyes and pulsing jugular vein.

---

blood type

TASTE: Robust and gamey with a strong finish. Pairs well with adrenaline, so hit that treadmill!

ATTRACTS: Playful, extroverted vampires who like open-top SUVs and enjoy sports.

WHERE YOU'LL FIND HIM: Standing up in the backseat of a jeep as his vampire crew rolls into the school parking lot.

blood type

TASTE: Bold and acidic with undercurrents of licorice. Fans of AB+ find the scent almost irresistible when the blood is slightly chilled, so leave the sweater in the car and master the sexy shiver for best results.

ATTRACTS: Rebel, bad-boy vampires.

WHERE YOU'LL FIND HIM: On a cross-country motorcycle trip through Romania. Start saving those frequent flier miles.

---

blood type

TASTE: Complex but smooth, with hints of honey and a surprising floral finish.

ATTRACTS: Melancholy, brooding vampires.

WHERE YOU'LL FIND HIM: Leaning languidly against a mossy tombstone in the local graveyard, absorbed in a volume of poetry. In order to snag one of these highly coveted yet elusive vampires, drape yourself dramatically across a nearby headstone and begin sighing mournfully. He'll be putty in your world-weary, tortured hands.

coaxing him out of the crypt

Now that we've established that you're the one for him and he's the one for you, there's the not-insignificant matter of making contact. Over the centuries, vampires have often been accused of playing hard to get—but, really, there's no playing involved. We're just hard to get. Still, fear not! With all the right words and all the right moves, you should be able to break his dawn.

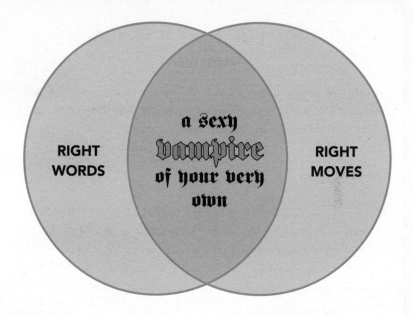

RIGHT WORDS

a sexy **Vampire** of your very own

RIGHT MOVES

You're feeling nervous already, aren't you? You're thinking, *Maybe it's better if I keep my distance. Maybe I should just love him from afar.* There's a small group of poets sitting in a lonely corner applauding that choice—but you deserve more than that. Your blood's going to boil until you talk to him, and the world's going to leave you cold until he's yours. Don't pretend you have any choice in the matter. Once you've found him, you have to see it through to the end.

Luckily for you mortal girls, actions and words aren't the only things that speak loudly to vampires. Unlike human boys, who can only focus on one sense at a time (and also seem to focus only on one anatomical feature at a time—or maybe two), vampires take in the whole picture. Often it's the combination of sensual messages that tips the balance from disinterest to love. Here we'll examine the best ways to catch your vampire's eye—or nose.

Scents that will drive a vampire wild

When you want a burger, you don't cover it in roses, do you? You shouldn't do that to yourself either—perfume only gets in the way. *These* are the scents a vampire can't resist!

❊ fear

Slightly sharp, slightly acidic, the smell of your fear will have your vampire doing fly-bys in no time. Try watching lots and lots of scary movies, or having your kid brother jump out from behind the couch when you don't expect it. Just remember to keep your hair back so the smell of fear on your neck isn't masked by the smell of your shampoo!

❊ desperation

This scent's a difficult one. You want to smell desperate to keep your fragile human life, not desperate to land a vampire boyfriend. Try thinking, *I'm going to die, I'm going to die.* Not, *I'm going to die single, I'm going to die single.* That should do the trick.

❊ adrenaline

Have you ran through the forest or stumbled terror-stricken through your house? Is your heart pounding and are your stomach muscles clenched? The zinc-like scent of adrenaline is pumping through your blood. Time for a sexy tussle!

❋ longing

Sweet, with a slight overtone of decay, the smell of your longing will intoxicate him. After all, who doesn't like to be loved? If you really want to reel him in, aim for hopeless longing—vampires report the scent is more complex and satisfying.

❋ blood

Ready to break out the big guns? Prick your finger and dab a little blood behind your ears, at your wrists, and especially in the hollow of your neck. This trick has been known to backfire, as it drives some vampires so wild that they actually kill you. But hey! It works at least half the time.

braun stein's tips for timeless beauty

I wouldn't know an eyelash curler from a torture device. My erstwhile colleague, Braun Stein, however, has been on the glamour scene since Elizabeth I started wearing makeup. Here are her words of wisdom for you:

Take that *Seventeen* magazine and chuck it right out the window (making sure, of course, not to hit the vampire who's hanging in the tree just outside). Those slick magazines are kids' stuff. You're in the big lair now.

✠ makeup

Keep it simple. When in doubt, ask yourself, "If I were stranded on a deserted tropical island, which three beauty items could I not live without?"

1. **SUNSCREEN, SPF 100 OR HIGHER.** (If you find yourself even mildly surprised at this suggestion, please give this book to someone who might actually use it.) Otherwise, you'll need to spend an extra three months holed up in your house, de-tanning, which may not be a lifetime for your vampire but will feel like it to you.

2. **FOUNDATION, PREFERABLY IN MOONBEAM.** (Those other whites just don't cut it.) You want to look pale, pale, pale, and slightly dew-kissed. Need we say more?

3. **CRIMSON LIPSTICK.** (And not that glossy, sparkly crap — we're talking the thick, solid stuff you can write love notes to your vampire on mirrors with — well, not literally).

✳ fashion

Got plaid? Spandex? Juicy Couture? Not anymore! Donate it all to charity—or, better yet, give everything to a girl who will never have *true* vampire appeal (unlike you!). The same goes for polo shirts, slouchy boots, slinky sweaters, and oversize tees. Nothing says classic vampire-chic like these timeless essentials:

❋ **VICTORIAN CORSETS.** The more plunging the neckline and the more stays to unlace, the better! Too cold, you say? Remember, gooseflesh is *hot*.

❋ **PUSH-UP BRA.** If you are well-endowed, good for you. If not, start saving! There's nothing like an enticing bustline to draw attention to your neck.

❋ **NOTHING SAYS NAUGHTY LIKE THAT PERFECT, SO-OLD-IT'S-THE-RAGE, VERSATILE PAIR OF LACE-UP ANKLE BOOTS.** *Ooh la la!* Of course, they are completely impractical for running through dark forests, but before you pass up these must-haves, remember that vulnerability is sort of the point.

❋ **IF YOU DO NOTHING ELSE, PLEASE (PLEASE, *PLEASE!*) AVOID WEARING PALE PINK, PALE BLUE, PALE YELLOW, PALE LAVENDER . . .** well, anything pale. Nothing says, "I'm translucent" like dark colors! And it should go without saying that you should stay away from patterns (paisley, stripes, etc.) like the plague. You don't want anything distracting him from your bustiered, pulsing, hot-blooded bod!

pickup lines

Once you've got the scent and got the look, you're ready to get your vampire.

The good news: You don't need a stake in order to find a way to his heart. You just have to make the first move.

Who, me? you're asking.

Yes, you.

Vampires don't make first moves. If we want you for food, yes. If we want you to date, no. It's just not in our nature.

Start by talking to him. Sometimes it can be as simple as a good pickup line.

these will work:

1. Do you know the way to the graveyard? I just died in your arms.
2. If looks could kill, Van Helsing would be out of a job!
3. Do you have a goblet ready? Because I cut my knee when I fell for you.
4. If I can't stop coughin', will you let me rest in yours?
5. Is that Purcell's "Funeral March" I hear, or is it just the sound of blood coursing through my delicious veins?

these won't work:

1. You're the garlic to my bread.
2. You light up a room. Will you be my sunrise every morning?
3. Bells were ringing when I met you.
4. You went straight to my heart like a silver bullet.
5. Is there a mirror in your crypt? I can see myself in there.

I do like it when the girl makes the first move. It's hard enough to date a human—the teasing I've endured from my fellow vampires can be extraordinarily cruel. So it's good to know you won't be rejected. And it's also nice to have such good access to blood.

—SIMON, 902

There's nothing sexier than heaving breath. I mean, if it sounds like there's a castle on her chest every time she breathes—wow. Hot. Also, if the blood smell is so thick I feel like I can lick it...yum.

—THEO, 112

The best thing is when I can save her—but not all the way. Like, the knife is flying through the air, and I manage to deflect it, but it still cuts off a little bit of her ear, so there's blood everywhere. Or she's tied to the train tracks and I swoop in and untie her except, oops, one of her legs is still stuck. I mean, I want her alive. But having blood everywhere is an added bonus—I mean, added beauty.

—GUSTAVO, 182

Surely you see a recurring theme here. You may not think of your blood as one of your more attractive features, but that's because you've been dating the wrong guys! If he's not going to appreciate you for your blood—it's the thing that gives you life, after all—then how is he truly going to appreciate anything else about you? By valuing your blood so highly, a vampire is saying, *I love the very core of you, the substance that courses through every single part of you.* He is loving you on a cellular level. And, yes, he's also hungry. But there's a reason he's talking to you instead of dining on you. And that, my dears, is love.

Still, not all vampires have the purest of interests. There is one telltale phrase that provides the perfect lens through which to view your vampire. We analyze it here.

"i want to suck your blood": an examination

So your conversation is going well . . . and then all of a sudden he drops, "I want to suck your blood." The only way to know whether you should swoon and fall deeply in love or grab your stake and run for the sun is by listening to which word he emphasizes. Here's a guide:

"i want to suck your blood."

He's an egotistical jerk. It's all about *his* needs. Don't expect to find eternal love with this demanding narcissist.

"i want to suck your blood."

Is it all about his wants? The only way to tell is to reply, "Well, I want to suck your face," and see if he kisses you. If he recoils in terror, this vampire's not for you. If his lips are soon on yours, get ready to cut garlic from your diet for a long, long time.

✻ "i want to suck your blood."

Does he want to gargle your blood? No. Does he want to use it to bake pies? No. Emphasizing the word *suck* is a sign of strong passion. The question is whether that passion is for you or just for your blood. Either way, though, it means he's totally interested in you, and that's awesome!

✻ "i want to suck your blood."

OMG! He's so into you and not just for your blood—he's into you as a person. Don't buy a black wedding dress just yet, but this could be true, eternal, everlastingly blissful love!

✻ "i want to suck your blood."

Ugh. Clearly, all this vampire cares about is your blood, not your brains. While it's nice to be wanted, this sounds like a one-way street to vampire heartbreak.

As the conversation continues, you might find yourself a little challenged. After all, a wise man (Proust? Liberace?) once said, "Talking with a vampire is very difficult." And he was absolutely right. It is very difficult. Let's face it—we vampires are older, wiser, smarter, more cultured, better traveled, better read, and more interesting than mortals. But don't despair! When vampires converse with humans, all we really want is for you to be dazzled by our brooding brilliance and refined tastes.

you must be ready to compromise some of your lesser human biases. While we want to see you smolder with a feisty sense of fierce independence, we don't want too much disagreement. For your conversation with your vampire to truly excel, I would suggest you work in a few of the following phrases:

❋ **"Yes! I'd love to go to Transylvania for spring break! I couldn't agree more that Acapulco would be horrible."**

❋ **"No, of course I understand that killing my brother was an accident. Don't worry about it—things like this are bound to happen."**

❋ **"I would love to hear another poem about me brushing my hair!"**

❋ **"My ex drove too slowly for me. I got so frustrated when he refused to break 150 miles per hour."**

❋ **"I totally want a pet bat. Do golden retrievers sleep upside down and use echolocation? Ha. Hardly."**

Not all girls are as quick on their feet (or with their tongues). Learn from the mistakes of your predecessors in the following testimonials.

I was at a pet shop when I saw this hot guy. I wanted to break the ice so I said, "Oh my God, these puppies are so cute, I could almost eat them!" But then he tells me the beagles are the most filling, and I totally ran away. In retrospect, I guess I should have been more open-minded.

—ABIGAIL, 16

Last Halloween, I was at a party and I saw this total hottie by the punch bowl—I mean, he was six foot one and rocking this Dracula costume that he totally couldn't have bought at Target. So I went to "get some punch" and complimented him on his amazing costume and he goes, "Honey, this isn't a costume, it's vintage Armani from Transylvania." How embarrassing!!

—TRUDY, 15

I thought Sebastian was into me, but I worried it was going to be a *century* before he asked me out. So when I skinned my knee, I walked around my yard and left little blood markings for him. Sebastian *still* hasn't called, and now my dog and my little brother are missing. I am so grounded.

—LINDSAY, 17

love at first date

ven immortals get nervous before first dates. Granted, we don't get as nervous as you do. Our palms don't sweat. Our stomachs don't fill with butterflies. We never, ever blush. But if we care enough to go on a date, we care about how it goes. Plus, we love how the nervousness raises your blood pressure. That's hot.

Your first hurdle, of course, is figuring out where to go and what to do on your date. It can't be too overwhelmingly romantic, but it can't seem too casual either. Walk the line carefully.

A NOTE FROM GRETA, A VAMPIRE SLAYER

No matter what I say, you're still going to go out with him, right? If you insist on going, please be sure to use protection!

- ❧ **Garlic spritz.** Take some garlic and put it in a spray bottle with some water. If he gets a little out of control, this will work even better than mace.

- ❧ **Holly.** Just a little sprig can make all the difference.

- ❧ **A small bell.** Yeah, the waiter might think you're summoning him over. But a ringing bell will also get your date's hand off your knee or his knee off your neck, if need be.

- ❧ **Pocket mirror.** If he's showing you something you don't want to see, show him something he doesn't want to see. Also good for fixing makeup.

- ❧ **A cross.** You might want to keep this in a pocket, so you don't have to rummage through your purse for it.

vampire-dating etiquette

Vampires aren't like other boys (but that's why you're attracted to them!), so don't expect them to act like everyone you've dated before—boys with pathetic carnations and their even more pathetic excuses. When dating a vampire, you must keep the following in mind:

promptness ❄ You should always be on time, but be aware that your vampire will likely show up late. He's been around for centuries, so chances are that minutes and hours don't mean much to him.

---

dining ❄ Try to plan a date that's not about eating, such as bowling, watching a movie, or another leisure activity that involves a cavernous room with no windows. But if eating does come up, be thoughtful. Skip the salad and order a steak cooked rare.

---

conversation ❄ Your boy has been around, so do a little studying. Create flash cards to help you memorize the kings and queens of Europe of the past 500 years, and make sure you're well-versed on Romanian politics of the 1600s. One thing you do not want to ask about is how many people he's eaten. It's really not polite to bring up murder on a first date.

---

other women ❄ Is the waitress flirting with him? Try not to hiss. Instead, "accidentally" tip over your water glass. As she's effortlessly carrying big trays around, you're covered in icy water. Who is more likely to need her life saved on a regular basis? Yeah, you won that round.

o give you an illustration of what your date might be like, I've decided to let you be the bat on the wall during the first date between a mortal girl and an immortal soul. Bridget, 17, is a high school senior from Millburn, New Jersey, where she is a member of Safe Rides and the Millburnettes singing group. Flavian, 212, is an accomplished writer and philatelist, and recently ended a long relationship. These are their stories.

🕸 BRIDGET 🕸

I was super nervous about my date with Flavian. I'd heard that he hadn't been on a date since his ex-girlfriend died from consumption in 1902, so I thought I should rock the whole vintage look, to keep it familiar. I wore this awesome high-necked lace dress but added some modern touches. I wanted to create an impression of timelessness, you know? Like, "Check me out. I'd be hot in any century!", in case he wants to transform me someday.

Flavian picked me up in his BMW, which was really cool, but I totally tripped walking across the driveway! It was sooo embarrassing. I hoped he didn't think I was a klutz.

He took me to dinner, which was nice of him since he can't, you know, eat. The conversation was pretty interesting. Flavian told me about growing up in the nineteenth century and how people argued all the time because you couldn't just bust out Wikipedia on your iPhone and be all like, "I *told* you the leeches were a bad idea."

Then things got a little weird. Flavian stopped talking and just sort of stared at me while I ate. I thought there might have been food in my teeth, so I went to the bathroom to check. On my way back to the table, I passed a group of guys from school, which was awesome because I knew that now *everyone* would know I went out with a vampire. (I totally got to sit in the wobbly chair at the end of the popular table the next week!)

When I got back to the table, though, Flavian got a funny look on his face. He slammed some money on the table, grabbed my hand, and dragged me out of the restaurant. When I asked him what was wrong, he told me that those guys had been thinking "disgusting" things about me. (P.S. Flavian can totally read minds.) I thought it was kind of sweet that he felt so protective, although I would've liked a few more bites of my burger.

We got back in the car and Flavian drove me home. He kissed me on the cheek (so gentlemanly!) and said good night. I had a nice time and would love to see him again, but I couldn't really tell if he was interested. I guess I'll just have to wait and see!

❧ FLAVIAN ❧

When I saw Bridget in that hideous turtleneck dress, I groaned. For a vampire, that's the equivalent of showing up for a date wearing a burlap sack. So I wasn't really feeling it at first. But then she tripped on the way to the car. I was immediately struck by her fragility. She was so lovely and delicate, totally unfit for a world full of dangers like gravel driveways and concealed sprinkler heads. I suddenly realized that I had to protect her. I would be her guardian against all things evil, like shoes with poor traction.

At dinner, I was captivated by the sight of her eating, watching those potentially deadly morsels of food travel down her lovely throat. At any moment, one of them could've become accidentally lodged in her trachea, so I decided to stop talking and focus on her swallowing so I could be prepared to perform the Heimlich maneuver at a moment's notice.

When Bridget came out of the bathroom, she passed a table full of vile, loathsome human boys whose heads were full of the foulest thoughts. This one little worm remembered that Bridget liked Frisbee and thought about inviting her to join the Ultimate Frisbee Club at school. It was utterly sickening. The idea of my precious angel surrounded by deadly flying discs! What if one were to crush her windpipe? Or strike her temple? I was incensed and had to remove Bridget from the restaurant before he got any other repulsive ideas in his moronic head.

I drove Bridget home and, after I was sure she was safely inside, ran around to the back of the house and scaled a tree in her yard. I've sat there for the past three nights, watching over her lest some misfortune befall her. I almost intervened when she stood on a chair to hang a picture (what if she had fallen?!), but I resisted. Tomorrow, I'm going to give her the eighty-page epic poem I wrote in honor of her beauty. I just need to find a phrase that rhymes with "ravishing nostrils" so I can finish the last stanza.

I t is always important to remember that the rules of dating have changed since your vampire was fifteen (for the first time). Take it slow. Remember, he's into chivalry and old-fashioned courtship. Still, don't be afraid to take risks. If he tries to hold your hand, just think really warm thoughts and go for it!

To help you even further, I've gathered some testimonials from human girls and vampire guys about some of their most memorable dates — memorable for being total disasters!

Wolfgang was one of those jumpy, paranoid types. He wasn't a cool, relaxed vampire like the ones you see on TV. We were eating at a nice restaurant and were about to order from the menu when I casually mentioned, "I think I'm going to have the steak." Well, Wolfgang didn't hear the first part, only the word *stake*. He jumped up and made such a scene as he stormed out of the restaurant. It was a mistake anyone could have made!

—DELILAH, 17

I showed her my teeth and she showed me the door.

—NICHOLAI, 333

I will *never* go on another blind date without asking about his "mortality status" ahead of time!

—REESE, 15

Vampires don't line dance. End of story.

—EUSTON, 492

Vampires are known for their straightforward way of speaking. While human boys' words can have all the solidity of squirming flesh, ours are like polished pieces of marble. Still, while what we say is clear enough to us, sometimes your human ears have a hard time hearing what we mean. This is something we investigate throughout the book, but here I would like to focus on dating language. As you've seen already, a phrase as straightforward as "I want to suck your blood" can have a multiplicity of meanings—so it's important to be sure you are understanding correctly. It can be a matter of life and death.

dating language: what he says and what it means

HE **says**: "You look delicious tonight."
HE **means**: "You look lovely tonight."

�֍ **This may seem a little odd, but it's really the highest compliment he could pay you.** Smile and say thank you. Do not tell him he looks delicious as well—that makes no sense. Instead, say, "I'm very taken by you, too."

HE **says**: "Let's go somewhere dark, quiet, and isolated."
HE **means**: "I want to get to know you better."

✖ **Now, if a mortal boy said this on a first date, you'd think he was a total creep.** But if a vampire says this, he's actually being really sweet. He just wants to get to know you better, in the dark. There's nothing weird about it at all. He'll be able to see you better that way. It's a sign the date is going well and that he's interested in you (or your blood).

HE says: "I'm not really looking for a girlfriend."
HE means: "I just want to make sure you're not after my power to give you immortality."

Vampires have to be careful—sometimes girls will use them in order to become undead. So when a vampire says this, he doesn't really mean that he doesn't want a girlfriend. Actually, he likes you a lot, and he's just trying to play it cool so that you will like him even more. And your willingness to wait means that you aren't looking for a one-night changeover-to-the-eternal. Consider this a sign the date is going very well!

As a rule, vampires do not gush. We leave it to the open veins to do that. So when you get to the end of the date, don't expect to know right away what he's thinking. If he hasn't devoured you, that's a good sign. If he says he'd love to hang out some other night, that's even better. He's not going to put on a goofy smile, or start calling you by a nickname. That's not vampire style, and the minute you start expecting that, you're sure to be disappointed. Instead, let him express himself in vampire ways. He might not text you before you get home, or show up at your locker the next morning with flowers. But there are still definite ways you can tell whether your date was a success or a bust.

love meter

❋ **hot!** He lunged for your neck before the appetizer arrived, then gazed longingly as he promised you eternity.

❋ **warm** He only went for your neck *after* you mentioned your blood type and only said he liked the same horror films as you *after* you said you liked them first.

❋ **chilly** He was only interested in talking about the things that he wants to do for an eternity and kept mentioning his last girlfriend, who he was with for almost 200 years.

❋ **cold** While you were talking with him, he was checking out other necks.

⊷ decoding the first kiss ⊷

The greatest reward a vampire can bestow at the end of a first date is the elusive first kiss. There's no middle ground here—none of that mixed-message hugging and/or handshaking and/or punching-on-the-arm that human boys can do. Either he simply walks away or he goes for it.

When it's all over and you've said good-bye . . . run home and turn to this page, so you can decode what just happened!

 ❋ **forehead kiss** In the world of human boys, the forehead kiss ranks up there with him saying, "So, your best friend thinks I'm cute?" Fear not, dear girl, as it is most certain that the forehead kiss your vampire just gave you means, "All the better to smell the delicious aroma wafting up from your exposed, pulsing neck." **Stay tuned—there's definitely more to come!**

 ❋ **hair kiss** You might think the hair kiss is your vampire being sweet and lightly romantic. In reality, your heart rate should be soaring higher than it does when you're working out with your mother's StairMaster on the "butt buster" setting. **This is the kiss that says, "Come closer, my pet!"**

 ❋ **ear kiss** Don't be seduced by this, perhaps the most tempting and distracting of kisses. Beware! Your vampire, unfortunately, is not paying attention to you; he's simply listening very (very!) intently to the flow of your hot, salty blood pulsing through your eardrums. **Proceed with caution.**

✳ **lip brush** Was it accidental? We don't think so! With vampires, *nothing* is accidental. **Give yourself a high five, for this is considered to be one of the most erotic vampire kisses.**

 ✳ **slip of the tongue** Things are moving fast. **You should be asking yourself, "If he's willing to exchange saliva, is blood next?!"**

 ✳ **neck nuzzle** This, of course, is the grand slam of vampire kisses. If you must question this kiss or its intentions, we recommend that you go back to chapter one of this book and start all over again. Otherwise, consider yourself sealed with his kiss! If he starts roaming, it's time to reassess your technique. If he stays in one place, honey, you've got true undead appeal! Not only is he going for you—he's also willing to hold back for you. **Pay close attention to what comes before and after.**

The neck nuzzle followed by the ear kiss: He's bored.
The neck nuzzle followed by the forehead kiss: Thumbs down, girlfriend. He already knows what's there and he doesn't like what he smells.
The hair kiss followed by the lip brush followed by the neck nuzzle: Start saying good-bye to your friends and family!

f you've survived the first date with both your life and his love intact, then you're ready to take it to the next level: a full-on relationship. In the next part, we'll show you how to navigate these treacherous (and sometimes bloody) waters.

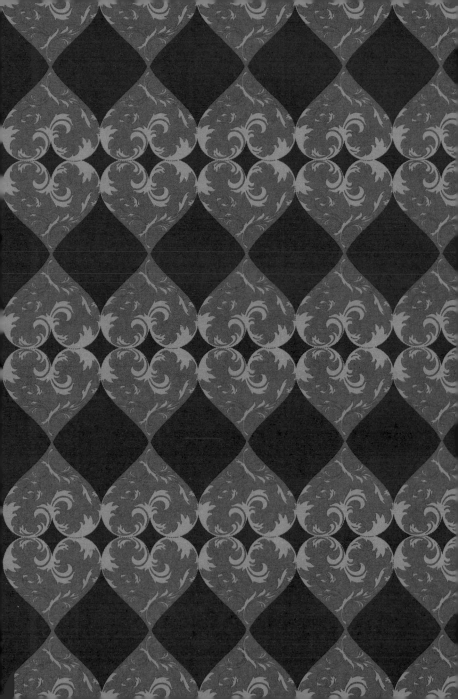

✤

now that you've got him, keep him!

vampires are from transylvania, girls are from pennsylvania

You've gotten one foot in the crypt—now you need to make sure that you can keep the allure going. Even if we vampires know immediately that we're going to be hopelessly devoted to you, we're not the types to actually blurt this out. Instead, we are firm believers in courtship—keeping enough distance for mystery, but not enough distance for misery.

Don't rush things. Whether it's a week from now or two centuries from now, you'll look back fondly on these euphoric nights of flying through the air—and these comforting days of staying indoors with all the window shades closed, watching old movies and curling up on the couch. Love isn't just found in the loud moments of sweeping statements and prolonged peril. It can also be found in the simple, small acts of getting to know each other.

I can hear your quavering, unconfident words in my ear: *Vlad, how can I possibly be good enough for a vampire? When will he realize that I'm just an ordinary girl while he is a sterling, brazen, hard-core rhapsody of undead perfection?*

I will not lie to you—he's got a lot going for him that you simply don't. But that hardly means the game is over before it's begun! Once you've won his heart, you gain control of the situation. We call this *blood-tied*—when a vampire is willing to forgo his superior knowledge, vast experience, supernatural power, and movie-star looks in order to possess the affections of a human girl. If you can get him there, he's yours, all yours, and all your underwhelming talents will be forgiven, obscured by the blaze of his undying devotion.

The key here is for you to keep it interesting, and to never make your inferiority to him *too* apparent. In that department, I am your humble advisor and (more often than not) sole hope.

First, let's start off with the undeniable fact that he is much, much older than you. I know this is something you don't want to think about—who wants to hook up with someone the age of her great-great-great-grandfather?—but luckily his shockingly young, good looks will make you forget the fact that he's older than any building you've ever been in (unless you travel internationally). If he's doing such a good job of seeming less-than-old, you have to hold your own in seeming more-than-young. Here are some guidelines that can help.

ten tips for dating a much, much, much older man

—◦◦◦◦—

Your vampire might give you a blank look when you mention *High School Musical* . . . or toasters. In order to minimize misunderstandings and maximize your vampire appeal, take a look at these tips.

---

1 ❈ start reading

How many centuries can vampires spend listening to humans ask the same inane questions? *Do I look fat in this toga/corset/velour jumpsuit? Where do you want to eat after the public execution/theater/movie?* Go to the library and ask for the book that's never been checked out. You can dazzle him with your knowledge of firefly mating habits!

---

2 ❈ be active

Your vampire has dated the hottest girls of the past three hundred years... but don't let that intimidate you. Sure, those girls spent four hours a day grooming, but trust me, it got *really* boring watching them do needlepoint all day. Showcase your vitality by joining a sports team and inviting your vampire to your games, or anything else that gives you a rosy flush.

---

3 ❈ use fuzzy math

If your mom confronts you after your vampire mentions something about the Reagan administration or the War of 1812, be prepared to explain, "Well, Bertram is two years older than me, which means he was born in 1798. Hey, what's for dinner?"

4 ❖ learn about his past

It would be super awkward to invite your vampire to tour Gettysburg if it turns out he, um, left mortality behind during the Civil War. Avoid forcing him to relive painful moments, like bloody wars or the time he missed an early opportunity to invest in Microsoft.

---

5 ❖ watch a ton of *masterpiece theatre*

I'm not claiming that Mr. Darcy was a vampire, but period pieces will explain some of your vampire's odd behaviors, like why he challenged your lab partner to a duel after he "dishonored" you by keeping the pencil you lent him.

---

6 ❖ keep your discussions to the present

If you start reminiscing about way back when you were ten, it'll only make him feel old. And at the same time, if you start talking about what you're going to be when you grow up, it'll also depress him — since he's never going to get to experience his twenties, thirties, forties, fifties, sixties, and so on. Not in the appropriate body, at least.

---

7 ❖ trash the hot pants

Remember, when your man was growing up, girls who flashed too much ankle were considered major hussies.

---

8 ❖ teach him to embrace technology

Skyping from the comfort of your coffin is much less taxing on the patience (not to mention the hair) than hanging out in bad weather.

9 ✥ give original gifts

Over the years, he's been given dozens of framed pictures, hundreds of poems, countless locks of hair, and possibly an albino peacock or two. Angelina Jolie thought she was being all original when she gave Billy Bob a vial of blood. Your vamp probably dated her great-great-grandmother and still has the blood to prove it. To make sure you're giving him something he's never received, keep it personal and try making it yourself!

---

10 ✥ be a twenty-first-century woman

He might have grown up in an age when any woman who knew the square root of 64 was burned at the stake for witchcraft, but that doesn't mean you should abandon your feminist principles. Saving you from falling into a curiously placed nest of vipers? Fine. Scooping you up in his arms to carry you over cracks in the sidewalk? Not so much.

I need a girl to make me feel young again. You know, when you can't look in a mirror, sometimes you lose track of how strikingly virile you look. You start to feel your age instead of looking it. So if a girl can reflect your youth back at you she's a keeper. Until she starts to grow old, of course. Then she's a downer.

—AJAX, 832

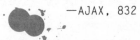

the most common mistakes when dating a vampire

Vampires are hard to get, but they're also notoriously hard to keep . . . at least until you hold them spellbound with your luscious, vulnerable mortality. To make this process easier, there are common mistakes that you can avoid when dating a vampire.

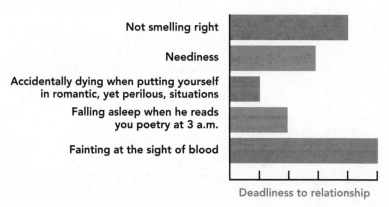

Not smelling right

Neediness

Accidentally dying when putting yourself in romantic, yet perilous, situations

Falling asleep when he reads you poetry at 3 a.m.

Fainting at the sight of blood

Deadliness to relationship

I want a relationship to be like a snake biting its tail—you don't know where one person begins and the other one ends, only that it's a seamless circle of devotion, with blood and teeth and pain thrown in at some point.

—CASSIUS, 112

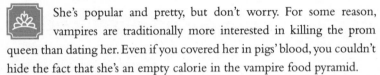

✦ your competition ✦

When you're first starting to date, it's important for you to know who—and, if it's a different species, what—you're up against when you're competing for your vampire's affections.

✦ prom queen

 She's popular and pretty, but don't worry. For some reason, vampires are traditionally more interested in killing the prom queen than dating her. Even if you covered her in pigs' blood, you couldn't hide the fact that she's an empty calorie in the vampire food pyramid.

THREAT LEVEL: LOW

✦ head cheerleader

 Athletic, powerful, and full of pep, the head cheerleader *would* be tough competition. Luckily, vampires tend to avoid cheerleaders because so many of them are secretly slayers.

THREAT LEVEL: LOW

✦ drama club chick

Full of angst and with a keen appreciation of beauty, the drama club chick will sometimes catch your vampire's eye. But usually not for long—she loves the limelight, but clearly *he* must play the starring role in any relationship.

THREAT LEVEL: MEDIUM

✣ student council president

Perky isn't usually what vampires go after, but don't dismiss the student council president too quickly. Her earnestness will amuse him, and he'll find the naïveté of her small, human ambitions kind of, well, adorable.

THREAT LEVEL: HIGH

✣ female vampire

She's so beautiful that you must shade your eyes against the glare of her perfection. She's seen centuries of suffering so she totally gets his broodiness, and she doesn't secretly find his crypt just a little bit creepy or need four cups of coffee to stay up all night. Sad little mortal girl, you can't hope to hold his attention if his eye strays to a female vampire.

THREAT LEVEL: VERY HIGH

✣ new girl

You don't see what's so special about her, with her clumsiness, her muttering, and her inability to stay alive without careful monitoring. But vampires can't resist the scent of new blood. Your only hope is that all those near-death experiences finally catch up with her, and she breaks her neck before he breaks your heart.

THREAT LEVEL: RED ALERT!

I can't tell you how many times girls have come up to me and said, *Vlad, how can I do this? I am not worthy!* Every time, I just slap their pretty little faces and say, "Do not snivel! Sniveling is unbecoming! You have beauty! You have blood! You have other qualities that aren't readily apparent to me right now! Buck up!"

getting to know your vampire's needs

Every relationship involves compromise. On your side, at least. If you want to be with a vampire, you have to embrace some of your differences . . . and compensate for your weaknesses by accommodating his strengths.

✤ Sleep

He doesn't need sleep, and *you* don't want to be thought of as a snooze. In the first heady months, he might occasionally enjoy watching you sleep. But it's always more fun if you fake-sleep instead, "accidentally" murmuring his name while arching your neck. (Do I really have to tell you how to play the game?)

However, I know the weak little flesh vessel that is your body needs downtime . . . so what to do? The answer, my mortal friend, is catnapping and caffeine.

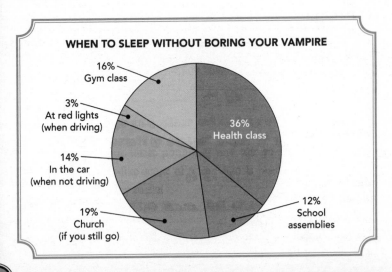

WHEN TO SLEEP WITHOUT BORING YOUR VAMPIRE

- 16% Gym class
- 3% At red lights (when driving)
- 14% In the car (when not driving)
- 19% Church (if you still go)
- 36% Health class
- 12% School assemblies

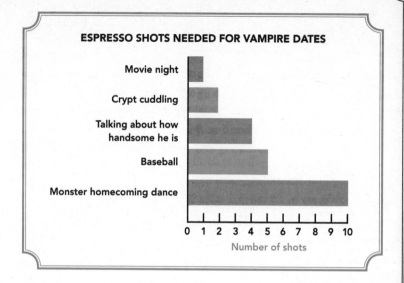

ESPRESSO SHOTS NEEDED FOR VAMPIRE DATES

Movie night
Crypt cuddling
Talking about how handsome he is
Baseball
Monster homecoming dance

0 1 2 3 4 5 6 7 8 9 10
Number of shots

✳ blood

Is there a local slaughterhouse nearby? Good. Put on a raincoat and plan to spend some time on the killing floor. You're going to need to build up your gag reflex if you're in love with a bloodsucker. Nothing will put your vampire off his tasty blood meals faster than a mortal girl puking in the background.

✳ cold

You are a fiery 98.6 degrees, but he is one cool customer. You want to spend eternity snuggled in his arms, but it's cold. Arctic, icy, frigidly cold. Your body will be tempted to shiver, but don't. There's nothing sexy about a hypothermic girlfriend. So start your cold-tolerance training now. Begin by cranking the AC, then move on to cold showers. By the time you graduate to ice baths, he might just find you tolerable.

❖ cooking for your vampire ❖

You don't always have to go out with your vampire—some of the best dates can be had at home. Not your home, of course—except for the visits to your bedroom in the middle of the night (just to watch!), he doesn't really like hanging out at your place. So instead of your crib, it's time for you to visit his crypt—and show him you can whip up a nice meal.

We all know there's only one substance that can give your vampire the calories he desires. Burger King and the Olive Garden just don't cater to a vampire's needs . . . unless the guy behind the counter has a big, open cut. When it comes to eating, think of your vampire as a kid who's got a lot of weird food allergies. If you make one of his favorites, however, he won't be able to resist taking a bite of your perfectly prepared delicacy. Here are some recipes that will make him feel like he's eating out of Mom's cauldron in Transylvania.

NOTE: These are for vampires only. Don't try them yourself!

❖ blood orange smoothie

What's in a name? Um, hello, only his favorite ingredient ever! Not to mention, it's as refreshingly cold as his heart. This tasty treat can be made *sans sang* so you both can enjoy, but add the real thing to get his taste buds tingling.

INGREDIENTS

1 cup hemoglobin, without pulp (or orange juice)
1 blood orange, peeled and cut into sections
½ cup plain yogurt
1 cup crushed ice

---

1. Mix hemoglobin or orange juice (boring!) and blood orange in a blender until orange is pulped.
2. Blend in yogurt.
3. Slowly add half of the ice and blend well. Pour in the rest of ice and blend until creamy.
4. Enjoy!

black pudding

Since blood is a key component of this sausage (and the best sausages are made with *fresh* blood), he'll definitely want to dig his fangs into this. Black pudding is one of the best comfort foods you can give him . . . aside from your jugular.

INGREDIENTS

2 pints blood (lamb, pig, or damsel, if available)
½ lb. suet
1 medium onion, finely chopped
1 pint milk
1 cup cooked barley
1 cup dry rolled oats
Pinch of salt and pepper
Sausage casings

1. Preheat oven to 300° F.
2. Mix ingredients (except casings) together in a large bowl.
3. Stuff sausage casings.
4. Fill baking pan halfway with water.
5. Bake sausages in pan in oven for 1½ hours.
6. Serve hot, chilled, or grilled.

✳ virgin bloody mary (TRADITIONAL VERSION)

Don't remind him of the historical implications of the drink's name. He might associate Queen Mary I, the drink's alleged namesake, with burnings at the stake. Just in case any of his friends or relatives suffered this fate, savor the flavor, not the history!

INGREDIENTS

1 cup tomato juice (or blood)
½ cup lemon juice
¼ tsp. Worcestershire sauce
⅛ tsp. hot sauce (not too hot—remember, he has sensitive taste buds!)
Salt and pepper to taste
Ice cubes

1. Combine all ingredients except the ice in a mixing glass.
2. Shake, then strain into a chilled glass over ice cubes.
3. Bottoms up!

✳ virgin bloody mary (VAMPIRE VERSION)

INGREDIENTS

1 virgin named Mary

1. Drain.
2. Serve.

decoding texts and emails

<hr/>

You should be enjoying yourself at this point—after all, you have the ideal companion to join you as the days count down to your inevitable death. But is he into it? It may be hard to tell, because until a vampire's completely smitten, you can't count on him to proclaim his everlasting devotion every time he likes the movie you chose or the joke you made.

In the absence of verbal compliments, you have to rely on the trail of words he leaves in his texts and emails.

✳ text messages

HE texts: Oh my most fragile of human darlings, I cannot bear to be apart from you a moment longer. I will scale the highest peaks to find myself once again in your arms.

HE means: Where r u?

<hr/>

HE texts: I am in agony, torn between my love for you and fear that I cannot restrain myself. Your flesh beckons like a glowing hand in oppressive darkness. I must stay away.

HE means: I'll call u later

<hr/>

HE texts: Busy 2night. Call u 2morrow.

HE means: I found someone better. Her blood makes yours smell like decaying cabbage. Peace out, human.

I heart your blood.

✴ e-mails

My dearest,

Tonight I am in one of the old family chalets in the mountains, missing you—I yearn for your nearness like the ocean does the moon. The mist has shrouded my windows in shadow, but high above the peaks, the stars glitter like the eyes of so many thirsty vampires. Hunting these past few days has been a plentiful and pleasant sport—indeed, passing the time here is always entertaining, and we have decided on extending our stay just a while longer. I long to hold you close to me and hear your delicate heart beating, Dearest, and look forward to doing so anon. Until that precious hour, I remain

Yours,

Gareth

Dearest of all? Sneak a peek at his other correspondence to see if he reserves this salutation only for you, or if he also calls his dentist "dearest."

He doesn't mention the specific country, precluding any snooping via Google Earth. Sneaky!

Poetic simile—good sign.

He sounds disappointed, but vampires like fog, and love anything to do with shrouds.

He's been craving a blood type other than yours! Not a good sign.

He's definitely not there alone!

READING: This vampire isn't alone. He's drinking blood that isn't yours, and he hasn't told you where he is or when he'll be staring in your window again. You have plenty of cause to be suspicious, but before you go angrily confronting him, take a few deep breaths. There's nothing vampires hate more than a controlling human! Well, except those cheapskates at the blood bank who refuse to give free samples.

❧

You are lucky because you have one thing a vampire male will never have: feminine intuition! You need to use it now to figure out if your casual dating is becoming more of a formal romance. Has he begun to follow you everywhere? Does he show up even when you think he's at least an hour's drive away? When you stub your toe, is he there instantly to carry you to your next class? When another girl bullies you, does she end up dead by next period? Yes, if a human boy were to do this, you'd call it stalking. But if a vampire does it, it isn't creepy! It's a great sign of his undying interest.

Still, it's one thing to go out on a few dates every now and then, and quite another to commit to a real relationship. Once you start calling him yours, there's a lot that comes with the territory. Don't get me wrong—it's a thrilling territory to be in. But you enter at your own risk. Are you ready for that?

are you ready to take it to the next level?

So you've been going out for a month or so and things are getting ~~hot~~ cold and heavy. He comes over for dinner (you eat, he watches), and you've begun flossing religiously to make sure those incisors last forever. But is your everlasting love just in your mind, or are you about to become the Brangelina of the undead?

Do the math to see if you and your vampire are ready to spend a century together—or if you won't make it past sunset tomorrow—by seeing which statements in the following columns apply most closely to your relationship.

CHECK THOSE THAT APPLY TO YOU FROM **column a**

_____ At Macy's, you always contemplate purchasing the extra-warm thermal gloves to keep your hands warm for all that sugary sweet hand-holding!

_____ You have timed your kisses down to a T to avoid anything over ten seconds—the danger zone. How romantic!

_____ You've gotten rid of the "I eat more solid food than my boyfriend" complex you used to have when you first started dating.

_____ You both share a chuckle when they ask for his ID at R-rated movies.

_____ When you miss going to the prom, he says, "Don't worry—there will be at least five hundred others."

CHECK THOSE THAT APPLY TO YOU FROM ❄ column b

_____ His parents are still surprised to see you (alive) at their place.

_____ He sometimes slips and calls you by his ex-girlfriend's name (you'd think he would forget a girl he met three centuries ago).

_____ You're more accustomed to your cat's withering glare than his adoring gaze.

_____ You never discuss the future, like what you'll do when the next century comes around.

_____ When you call him late at night, he says he can't hang out because he's "tired."

❄ MOSTLY AGREE WITH COLUMN A

Okay, so you might have a couple of minor things to sort out, like that staring and stalking thing—but no problem! You two understand each other well and you've both shown signs that you're ready and willing to make this a healthy (sorta), normal (kinda), loving relationship.

❄ MOSTLY AGREE WITH COLUMN B

If you find yourself agreeing with more statements in Column B, wipe off that white foundation and get thee to a pep rally. It's time to re-enter the human world before your name is a faded entry in his little black book . . . or on a tombstone.

I f you've made it this far, it looks like you're ready to get serious with your vampire. The risks might just be worth it . . . *if* your vampire remains into you.

CHAPTER SIX

the blood pressure increases

ah, young love! Even though it hasn't happened to me in centuries, I can still remember the rush that comes from finding someone with whom to share a relationship. Nothing is better than the long conversations, the even longer walks, and the feeling that you are speaking a language that only the two of you can fully understand. Eternity pales in comparison. So naturally, you want to make the most of it when you have it.

I am 99% sure I can guess your reaction to the chapter title: *Vlad, what do you mean by taking it to the next level?* I'm not talking about anything sordid or sexual—the kind of thing human boys mean when they implore you to "take it to the next level." No, I'm talking the most important kind of intimacy here: the intimacy of souls. Humans and vampires are alike in one regard: *dating* and *loving* are not the same thing. You must now leave the realm of the former and attempt to attain the heights of the latter.

First, you and your vampire must have "The Talk," making it certain that neither of you is seeing any other people/vampires/werewolves/etc. You don't want him laying his hands (or teeth) on any other girl, and he doesn't want you slip-sliding into affairs with your classmates or any other supernatural swains who come a-courtin'. You must be honest here. Later, he will resist an eternity with one girl (see chapter nine), but when your love has a full bloom on its proverbial cheek, he will be too busy licking his lips for his eye to wander. (Try to make your eye wander while licking your lips—it's very, very hard to do.)

You will be tempted to create what Kurt Vonnegut once called "a nation of two." (Vonnegut wasn't writing about vampires when he coined this term, but I imagine he would have been amused to have it used in this context.) You know—or will soon—what it's like to be half the population of a nation of two; you want to be separate from everyone else, and can't understand why they won't just leave you and your vampire alone. You must resist this impulse. You're going to need your friends and family in the future, so don't ditch them too frequently now. You also need to get to know his friends and family—a scary prospect, I know, but an essential one.

Introduce Alaric to my friends—are you joking!?!
He may be a vampire, but my friends are the real
bloodsuckers. If they saw me with a hottie like
Alaric, suddenly they'd be all into neck exfoliation.
Who needs the competition?

—MANDY, 15

Meeting my ex-girlfriend's friends was the most
unimaginably boring, mind-numbing experience of the
last 150 years. We met in the food court of a mall,
so I had nothing to do but slump in my seat while her
little girlfriends and their boyfriends stuffed dead
meat into their faces. The piped-in music grated on my
sophisticated ears, and I don't think my sense of smell
was quite as keen for weeks thereafter. They didn't
want to discuss the state of the economy, politics
in Eastern Europe, or UN policies on global warming
with regards to either pole—in fact, they only seemed
interested in the "game" that was happening next week.
Insufferable. Plus, her friends wore such indecently
low-cut tops that it proved difficult, even with my
steely self-control, to do much else other than stare
at their enticing jugulars.

—TRISTRAM, 346

ten Strategies for meeting his friends

If your vampire wants to introduce you to his friends, it means he really likes you and has no immediate plans to drink your blood. (Vampires only introduce girlfriends, not casual flings or snacks.) It's important to make a good impression, though. His friends might not approve of him dating a human, so you have to show them that you have more to offer than a tender vein. Here are some tips.

---

1 ✤ TAKE A FEW DEEP BREATHS AND TRY TO SLOW YOUR HEART RATE. It's rude to approach a group of vampires with a racing pulse. It's like offering your friend a cupcake and then shoving it in your own mouth.

---

2 ✤ SPEAK SLOWLY. Compared to their languid reserve, your chatter will make you sound like a yapping Chihuahua. Speak in low tones and try to remove any hint of enthusiasm from your voice.

---

3 ✤ DON'T WORRY IF THE VAMPIRE GIRLS SEEM ALOOF. Or angry. Or like they want to shove a straw in your throat and turn you into a human Big Gulp. You know how senior girls always hate freshman girls who date senior boys? Now multiply that by three hundred (years) and you'll understand why Arabella and Imogen don't want to be besties.

---

4 ✤ FIND WAYS TO COMPLIMENT THE VAMPIRES ON SOMETHING OTHER THAN THEIR LOOKS. Feel free to tell Brutus you enjoyed his lute performance at the talent show. Or mention to Alastair how much you admire his work for the hemophiliac charity.

---

5 ❄ **BEFORE YOU MEET, GO ONLINE AND RESEARCH SOME LOCAL INDIE BANDS.** Vampires like all things underground, so make sure you have some great names to drop.

---

6 ❄ **IT'S IMPORTANT TO REMAIN CALM.** You never want to give off victim or prey vibes. Stand tall. Don't shift. Try not to blink excessively. Don't swallow too often. Don't flinch at loud noises. Actually. . . meeting a group of vampires is like encountering a hungry grizzly bear. Just play dead.

---

7 ❄ **WEAR LOTS OF BLACK.** It says "I also know what it's like to be deep and tortured. My black T-shirt totally reflects the darkness within. Or maybe it's the darkness without . . . ?" When in doubt, just scowl.

---

8 ❄ **LAUGH AT ALL THEIR JOKES, EVEN THE ONES ABOUT MAIMING HUMANS.** You don't want to come across as uptight!

---

9 ❄ **DON'T SWOON.** Yes, you might be surrounded by a sea of divine bodies, perfectly tousled hair, luscious sneering lips, and the irresistible air of haughty disdain, but keep it together.

---

10 ❄ **PEPPER THE CONVERSATION WITH NUMEROUS REFERENCES TO DEATH OR OTHER REALLY DEPRESSING TOPICS.** For instance, "That reminds me of that night I spent reading Emily Dickinson in the graveyard, contemplating the inevitability of death." Or, "Who wants to go check out that exhibition on plagues? I heard you can still see the look of anguish on the mummified corpses' faces!"

Introducing [my boyfriend] Tarquin to my family was great! They had no idea he's "mortality-challenged." Before he came over, I removed some crosses, tossed all the garlic in the garbage, and locked up Smoochie, our Pomeranian, just in case! Tarquin arrived wearing the outfit I had selected for him. I had swapped his cloak for a blue polo shirt that really brought out the shadows under his eyes!

My mom had invited Tarquin to join us for dinner. I told her he'd be happy to sit with us but that he couldn't eat because he's following a detox regimen he read about on Gwyneth Paltrow's blog. We almost hit a tiny road bump when my dad asked about Tarquin's college plans. Tarquin started to explain how he already has an MD, four master's degrees, and two PhDs, but I jumped in and changed the subject.

After dinner, we all played Pictionary, which went well until it was Tarquin's turn to draw. After a few minutes, I realized he was sketching a mangled corpse draped over the side of a coffin, so I said, "Oh! What a great canoe, Tarquie!" and made up a story about how Tarquin spends every summer taking underprivileged children on canoeing trips. My parents were really impressed!

—EMMA, 17

are you ready to introduce him to your family?

——⟊⟊⟊⟊⟊——

1. **When you talk about your parents, your vampire:**
   a. Looks nervous or curls his lip in disgust.
   b. Seems curious and asks questions.
   c. Doesn't change the expression on his chiseled marble face.

2. **Which phrase do you hear from your parents most often?**
   a. "What does your new boyfriend like best for dinner?"
   b. "Have a nice date, dear. Don't be home too late."
   c. "You haven't been home in weeks. You need to stop seeing this boy."

3. **You're worried about him meeting your sister because:**
   a. She'll make an idiot of herself flirting with him.
   b. They'll have nothing in common to talk about.
   c. Her neck is way prettier than yours!

4. **What's his relationship with his parents like?**
   a. They're very close—after all, the family that maims together stays together.
   b. They just don't understand their unbelievably hot, remarkably un-aged, thirsty son.
   c. Does he even have parents? He's never mentioned them. . . .

5. **What's the worst thing you can imagine about your vampire boyfriend meeting your parents?**

    a. Your parents will talk down to him (ignoring his obvious intelligence). Or worse, show him your embarrassing baby pictures!

    b. Nothing much. His great (if sarcastic) sense of humor will win anyone over.

    c. What if he slips and mentions that he watches you sleep every night?

6. **Which L-word has he used so far?**

    a. "Love," as in, "I love how much you admire my poetry."

    b. "Lunch," as in, "I'd love to have ~~you for lunch~~ lunch with you."

    c. "Love," as in, "You're my beloved."

7. **Dinner might be a disaster because:**

    a. It's so weird that everyone gets along—usually your parents hate your boyfriends.

    b. Your vampire ignores the cookies your mom baked for dessert and goes right for your big brother's jugular!

    c. Your dad asks point-blank why you'd told him not to cook with garlic that night.

8. **How long have you been dating?**

    a. Not long—just a few gorgeous, moonlit nights.

    b. Longer than your last relationship, but not eternity . . . yet.

    c. A couple of dangerous but exciting months!

✠ scoring ✠

TALLY UP YOUR POINTS FOR EACH ANSWER:

1. **a.** 0 **b.** 2 **c.** 1 **2.** **a.** 2 **b.** 1 **c.** 0 **3.** **a.** 1 **b.** 2 **c.** 0 **4.** **a.** 2 **b.** 1 **c.** 0

5. **a.** 0 **b.** 2 **c.** 1 **6.** **a.** 1 **b.** 0 **c.** 2 **7.** **a.** 2 **b.** 0 **c.** 1 **8.** **a.** 0 **b.** 2 **c.** 1

❄ FOR A SCORE OF 0 TO 5

No Pulse! Your parents don't like that you spend so much time with him. Your vampire boyfriend is completely turned off at the thought of your family. Why were you even *thinking* of introducing him to your family? For now, it's best to keep this relationship in the crypt and away from your kitchen table.

❄ FOR A SCORE OF 6 TO 11

Faint Heartbeat. Maybe your vampire's still too possessive to meet the other people in your life. Maybe your parents are still warming to the idea of you spending eternity with him. Either way, it's probably best to wait a little bit before bringing him home to dinner. Give him a few months (or a few centuries), and by then everyone should have warmed to the idea. Or they'll be cold in their graves. Whatever.

❄ FOR A SCORE OF 12 TO 16

Blood Pumping! You've made him fall so fangs over heels that he'd happily cross continents or fight an entire pack of werewolves for you . . . or even brave meeting your parents. And once he does, you're sure his unearthly good looks and velvety-smooth personality will charm them—maybe you'll finally get that dawn curfew you've been pushing for!

My dad never approved of me dating vampires. "They're not our kind! Vampires should stick with vampires, and humans should stick with humans," he'd say as he forbade me to bring one home. Then I brought home Will as "a friend." Dad and he got along so well they went out back and threw around the football! When I asked Dad afterward if it was okay for me to date Will he said, "Sure! He's awesome!" Clearly, he'd gotten over his prejudices against vampires now that he could put a (pale) face to one.

—HARMONY, 17

After exchanging manly displays of brute strength with Harmony's father, I told her mother that her nineteenth-century cabinet reminded me of my own mother's. Soon we were talking antiques while Harmony's dad fired up the grill. I took my steak extra, extra rare and let her father win when he challenged me to "a little arm wrestling" after the meal. They never even asked about the fangs.

—WILL, 254

ten things to avoid at all costs when you meet his family

You've known your parents your whole life. But his family…well, they were around for lifetimes before you. They've seen so many other girls come and go, oftentimes before they've even had a chance to digest her presence. Here is a list of ten things you should under no circumstances do during that first encounter.

1 ❋ **IF YOU ARE GOING TO TALK ABOUT CURRENT EVENTS,** keep to the national or global level. Discussing local news is always fraught with unfortunate implications (e.g., "Did you hear about that guy who was found dead by the river?" or "Have you seen those posters for a missing horse that are all around town?").

2 ❋ **DON'T JOKE ABOUT THEIR GLUM EXPRESSIONS.** One girl I knew reacted by asking, "Who died?" and soon, the answer was her.

3 ❋ **MAKE SURE NOT TO USE THESE WORDS AND PHRASES** during dinnertime conversation: *batty, bloodless, fang-happy, full moon, sunny disposition, vegetarian, Count Chocula.*

4 ❋ **IF YOU'RE GOING OVER TO HIS HOUSE FOR DINNER,** be sure to bring a host gift. Sadly, a jar of jam or a bottle of wine won't cut it. Think more along the lines of "ritual sacrifice"—going to a butcher shop, getting all of their "leftovers," and wrapping them in a nice floral tarp will always endear you to a vampire's family. Just be careful—don't

ever give them something you wouldn't want to chew yourself. Because if you refuse to eat what's put in front of you, you might become the main course.

---

5 ❄ **DRESS CONSERVATIVELY,** and if you have open cuts or sores, cover them with duct tape (unless they are on your face, in which case you should layer three Band-Aids crosswise to one another).

---

6 ❄ **NEVER EXPRESS TOO MUCH CURIOSITY** as to when and how your vampire was "born." Inappropriate questions include: "How did you know he was the one to make undead?"; "What was he like as a child . . . before you turned him into a vampire?"; and "They grow old so fast, don't they? . . . Except, of course, when they don't."

---

7 ❄ **DON'T ASK TO SEE FAMILY PHOTOS.** They don't have any. And if you want to take a photo as a souvenir, don't use your flash.

---

8 ❄ **ALWAYS CHECK WITH YOUR VAMPIRE BEFOREHAND ABOUT WHAT HIS PARENTS LIKE TO BE CALLED.** You might assume it's "Mr. and Mrs. Lestat," but it could end up that they are Sir and Madam, Monsieur and Madame, Duke and Duchess, Tzar and Tzarina, or simply Steve and Jo.

---

9 ❄ **WITH SIBLINGS, NEVER ASK WHO'S YOUNGER AND WHO'S OLDER,** because the whole issue is very confusing, and you don't want to have to clarify by asking, "Which one of you was killed first?"

---

10 ❄ **DON'T WEAR ANY CLOTHING WITH A PICTURE OF A KITTEN, PUPPY, PONY, ELEPHANT, OR BLOOD SAUSAGE ON IT.** (In general, this is a good rule for mortal society as well.)

Once you've gotten his and your friends and family welcoming the relationship, you can step back into the nation of two for a little while. If you want to be in this relationship for the long haul (and I mean a very long haul), you have to show him that it'll never be boring, and that he's still going to love you in 2109 the same way that he loves you now. No pressure!

likelihood that he will get tired of you

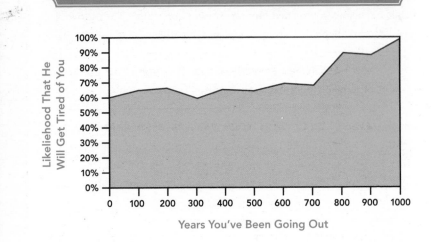

Years You've Been Going Out

If you're going to keep his interest, you're going to have to work it! *But Vlad*, some of you girls are whingeing, *that's a lot of work*! Well, princess, who ever told you that dating a vampire would be a jolly, easy thing? Not bloody me! You are asking to captivate the most eligible bachelor creature in all of creation—at the very least, you'd better be prepared to take up some new hobbies.

making your room more vampire-friendly

Tired of always going back to his crypt? Show him you want him to come over by making your room more vampire-friendly. Your design choices also offer a great opportunity to show off the qualities that make you an ideal girlfriend for a vampire.

windows

If you have any say in the matter, try to install windows that can be opened from the outside. Nothing will frustrate your vampire sweetie more than coming over to watch you sleep for an hour (or eight) and finding himself locked out.

bedding

Avoid thick comforters that muffle the exhilarating and delicious sound of your heartbeat. Depriving your vampire of that joy is like giving him earplugs at the symphony, or covering his nose as you pass a particularly gruesome car crash.

lighting

Dim the overhead light and invest in lots and lots of candles. The soft, flickering light will make you look deep and contemplative, even if you're really just trying to remember where you left your iPod charger.

✤ bookshelves

 Your books express a lot about you. A copy of *Romeo and Juliet* screams, "I'm all over the whole star-crossed lover thing. Tragic endings rock." *Wuthering Heights* suggests, "I'm totally into tempestuous romances. I love you! I hate you! I am you! Let's go mope on the moor." A well-worn copy of *The Picture of Dorian Gray* announces, "I am in no way turned off by men who trade their souls for eternal youth and beauty." The opportunities to manipulate your vampire are endless.

✤ clutter

Think "stark cave" when you're cleaning up. The more cavernous you can make your room feel, the more comfortable he'll be.

✤ airing out the crypt

Remember, your vampire is more sensitive than human boys. His nose will wrinkle at the scent of your "refreshing spring day" room spray, and your vanilla chai diffuser will have him clutching his stomach from nausea. If you want him to feel like he's relaxing in a desolate forest, try some musky smells instead. Mold, mildew, damp earth, and rotting leaves are crucial components of vampire aromatherapy.

✤ mirrors

You're just going to have to take his word for it when he compliments the luscious dark bags under your enchanting eyes. Mirrors are a big no-no, so throw them out with the clutter.

constructing the infinite vampire playlist

One of the best ways to show your vampire that you want to be with him always and forever is to make him a mix that he'll love for all eternity. The following songs should do the trick.

1. Annie Lennox, "Love Song for a Vampire"
2. Concrete Blonde, "Bloodletting (The Vampire Song)"
3. Suzanne Vega, "Blood Makes Noise"
4. Ash, "Vampire Love"
5. Vampire Weekend, "I Stand Corrected"
6. Coldplay, "A Rush of Blood to the Head"
7. Fright Ranger, "Oh Oh Oh Sexy Vampire"
8. Editors, "Blood"
9. Bon Iver, "Blood Bank"
10. Jonny Greenwood, "There Will Be Blood"
11. Say Hi to Your Mom, "These Fangs"
12. Arcade Fire, "Vampire Forest Fire"
13. Razorlight, "Blood for Wild Blood"
14. White Lies, "To Lose My Life"
15. Marilyn Manson, "If I Was Your Vampire"
16. Tori Amos, "Blood Roses"
17. Kronos Quartet, "The Crypt"
18. The Bangles, "Eternal Flame"
19. Rob Pattinson, "Never Think"
20. Evanescence, "My Immortal"★

★ *A Kidz Bop version is also available for this song, if your vampire is into that kind of thing.*

your warm heart, his cold shoulder

just like blood, love sometimes clots. And, yes, sometimes that's fatal, especially when your heart is involved. But other times the clot just passes, if you handle it the right way.

Vampire relationships are full of insecurity. (I hope I've never indicated to you otherwise.) It just comes with the territory. If you want to date a sexy, brooding vampire, you're going to end up lying awake at night asking yourself questions like *Are my veins big enough?* and *Does he still like my scent?* and *Why isn't he calling me back?*

Don't worry, though (at least not until we get to chapter nine). The ways of a vampire are mysterious and are bound to cause you some insecurity. Following are some common vampire behaviors that cause girls the most anxiety. If these behaviors normally freak you out, just remember, *it's not you; it's because he's a vampire.*

⚜ reading your vampire ⚜

❄ brooding

Is your vampire staring off into space with a forlorn look on his face? Is he unresponsive to your riveting story about what you and your best friend, Jenny, bought at the mall? Well, good! **That's what happy vampires do: They brood.**

❄ possessiveness

Is your vampire constantly jealous and possessive? When you're talking with a guy friend, does he show up unexpectedly and intimidate him? If so, that's great news! When human boys do this type of thing, it's usually because they're insecure jerks. **But when vampires do it, it means they love you!**

❄ laziness

Girls often mistake a vampire's desire to stay indoors during the day as laziness. Yeah, right. Would a lazy person really sprint from Boston to Montreal in the middle of the night just because he was craving some maple-flavored AB negative? **Your vampire's not lazy; he just doesn't want to go sailing with you and your friends.**

❄ not eating

It's not because he's upset or worried he's getting fat. It's just because he doesn't eat. **He drinks blood. You should know that by now.**

Communication is a two-way dark alley—there are behaviors of yours that he won't understand either. Navigate them carefully.

Who goes to get a drink from a cow and comes back
with milk?!? I will never understand humans.

—LEMUEL, 203

Why must humans always ask what's wrong? Nothing's
wrong—I'm a vampire! I'm supposed to be reserved
and moody.

—GUSTAVO, 182

Mandy's breathing is so loud. She does it over and
over and over again. I can't make her stop. (Well,
there is one way. . . .)

—ALARIC, 223

I keep telling her it's not my fault that I have
such good eyesight. The thing is, I can see every
little pore on Agnes's nose, and . . . well . . . I
find it rather revolting.

—WILHELM, 118

when is a cold shoulder more than just a cold shoulder?

It's important to know the difference between your vampire's basic irritation with your humanity and complete irritation with you in particular. Face it—you can't help being human, and odds are if he was willing to go for you in the first place, he must have found something charming about your mortal self. So if he has issues, you need to face them rather than blame them on the fact that you are a breathing, eating, defecating mess of a being. If you suspect that your vampire is losing interest, take this true-or-false quiz to find out what you should do.

1. When you ask him if he wants to hang out, he stares at the ground and mutters something about needing to study for his geometry test in case, you know, they've added some new shapes since the last time he was in tenth grade. **true / false**

2. You tell him you're going to start sleeping with the shades down and the window closed . . . and he doesn't seem to mind. **true / false**

3. He picks up his cell phone and shouts into it, "What? The house is on fire, the dog is stuck in a well, and you can't find the TV remote? I'll be there in a sec!" even when you never heard his phone ring. **true / false**

4. When you suggest a romantic roam through the mausoleum, he invites his friends along. **true / false**

5. You've noticed someone else's blood on his collar. **true / false**

6. If you mention eternity, he starts talking about booking a solo vacation to see his great-great-great-great-great-great-grandmother in Prague. **true** / **false**

7. He gave you an iPod for your birthday that includes the songs "Born to Run," "Miss Independence," and a scratchy-sounding track called "You're Too Sexy For Your Vampire." **true** / **false**

8. Your vampire has started texting you instead of calling or flying over in person. **true** / **false**

9. He won't hold your hand in public anymore because it's "too warm." **true** / **false**

10. Last week, he sent you a copy of *Little-known Supernatural Hunks: A Girl's Guide to Thinking Outside the Crypt.* **true** / **false**

✥⇒ Scoring ⇐✥

❋ IF YOU ANSWERED MOSTLY "TRUE"

Stick a stake in it, this relationship is just about done. Have you been coming in smelling like garlic, wearing pink shirts, or telling him you can lift heavy objects by yourself? Curb any independent behavior, and put away vampire repellents immediately. If the situation doesn't improve right away, it's time to slay this relationship (see chapter eleven).

❋ IF YOU ANSWERED MOSTLY "FALSE"

Are you sure *you* answered honestly? That weird stain on his collar wasn't chocolate, honey. Still sure? Well, then start planning for the future — he's thinking eternity! You can vamp up the vulnerability a little to accelerate the process, but he'll probably be ready to transform you soon!

what he says and what it means

If you want to know how the relationship is going, you have to pay attention to every word that falls from his stoic, dashing visage. Sometimes his language is dazzlingly straightforward (e.g., "I love you always and forever" or "It's time for me to kill you . . . all the way"). Other times, the meaning of his words might not be as clear. That's why it's good that you have a vampire like me to explain the meaning to you.

HE SAYS: "I'm really thirsty."

HE MEANS: "I think I need to see—or at least drink from—other people right now. Because if I wanted to have a nice long sip of you, I wouldn't be telling you I was thirsty, I'd be doing something about it."

HE SAYS: "You are as beautiful as moonlight."

HE MEANS: "I am going to restrain myself like a gentleman, but I want to ravage you like a beast."

HE SAYS: "You are my sunshine."

HE MEANS: "Girl, you're killing me! I need out. Right now."

HE SAYS: "I think I have cold feet."

HE MEANS: "Everything's normal. Let's keep dating."

HE SAYS: "Do you ever wish I was a werewolf?"

HE MEANS: "Once in a full moon, I can be insecure, too. Show me a little more that you love me."

romantic things he should be doing

It's important to figure out if he's a Romeo or a Romeoh-no-he-didn't! Here are the ways a vampire shows that if his heart *could* beat, it would beat for you.

1 ❄ watching you sleep

You are his little flower of human flesh, and he likes to spend every second listening to the song of your pumping blood—even while you sleep. So, no snoring, no morning breath, no embarrassing scratching.

2 ❄ buying you stuff

Little-known fact about vampires—they're *loaded* (especially if they come from Transylvanian nobility.) Chances are your vamp is sitting on a pile of treasure (often literally a pile of golden coins—he likes to roll around in them).

3 ❄ snuggling

Here's what you'll need: Two body-sized pillows (his flesh is like rock). One thermal blanket (his skin is like ice). Two heating pads (one for each foot). One woolly hat. Time to get cozy!

4 ❄ writing love ballads

He was probably friends with Shelley, and he speaks with adorably antiquated "thous" and "wherefores," so look no further if you want your mortal life compared to a fleeting sunset. Bonus points if he adds some guitar.

5 ❋ killing other people

He's hungry, but he's thoughtful. So he doesn't eat *you*, he eats your enemies!

---

6 ❋ Sharing his time

He follows you to class, he stays with you all night. He's there when you wake and when you sleep. You even have to ask permission to go to the bathroom! It's how you know you're really special.

---

7 ❋ taking you flying

The wind rushes by, the ground whirls beneath you. You're cold and slightly nauseated, but your friends are *totally* jealous! (Note: It will be mildly uncomfortable if he assumes bat form when he flies.)

---

8 ❋ talking eternity

You thought talking about spending eternity together was going to be really romantic, but instead, he's surprisingly practical. Instead of describing a little crypt in the woods, he's talking estate-tax loopholes.

---

9 ❋ taking you out to dinner

There's nothing more boring for a vampire than spending time in a restaurant. (Unless the waiter is going to be a snack.) So it's superspecial when he takes you out to dinner. Because human food isn't his thing. And small talk isn't either. And crowded places freak him out. So you had better appreciate this gesture!

But Vlad, you're saying, *what can I do to match the colossal greatness that is a vampire boyfriend? I can't give him warp-speed piggyback rides to class or kill his enemies (because they're already dead). I fear he'll think I'm not as romantic as he is!*

Well, yes, that's a perfectly valid fear. But don't make despair your middle name quite yet. You can:

❈ **SURPRISE HIM** by leaving a pile of sudoku books on your windowsill that will help him pass the time while you're asleep.

❈ **TAKE A BOX OF CHOCOLATES** and fill the squares with little bite-sized tastes of your own blood. For flavor variety, try eating different foods before you prick your finger. Want to show him your spicy side? Swallow a few spoonfuls of Tabasco sauce. Eager to reveal your sweet inner nature? Start gorging on honey!

❈ **CIRCULATE A PETITION TO BAN GARLIC** from all supermarkets and restaurants in your town.

❈ **TAKE UP SKYDIVING,** which will show him you're ready and willing to fall that extra mile, even in a movement-restricting corset.

❈ **SLEEP ALL DAY** and stay out with him all night. Yeah, your grades will plummet and you'll lose all your friends. But what's all that in the face of immortality? Your eyes will grow accustomed to the dark—and your heart will grow accustomed to the dark as well.

❈ **TAKE UP A NEW LANGUAGE,** like Romanian! If nothing else, learn these simple, everyday phrases: "Bite me," "Forever yours," "Rare, please," "My, what sharp teeth you have!"

❈ **WRITE HIM A POEM!** If you need help, use the guide on the next page.

poetry for your vampire

the fill-in option

Fill in each blank with the word that best describes your vampire and in a few minutes, you'll have a romantic poem he's sure to cherish forever (or at least until you've begun to decompose).

Dearest _____ ,
                your vampire's name

How I adore your _____ skin
                sparkly, rock-hard, smooth

From the tips of your _____ toes to your dazzling, exquisite chin.
                frigid, icy, chilly

I want to spend eternity inhaling your glorious _____ breath
                minty, fresh, floral

So please transform me before I succumb to human death!

When I look at you, my heart with _____ begins to flood
                love, longing, awe

I'll give you my soul, and every last pint of my _____ blood.
                sweet, spicy, savory

✦

Do-it-yourself vampire poetry!

If you want to go your own way, here are some helpful rhymes for you to use.

VAMPIRE
inspire, perspire, dire, lyre, fire, desire, flat tire

BLOOD
stud, flood, mud, scud (like the missile), cud

ETERNAL
infernal, vernal, internal, diurnal, paternal (although that might be a little weird)

COLD
bold, enfold, hold, foretold, gold (do *not* mention "old")

FANG
hang, sang, clang, kd lang, *Sturm und Drang* (look it up)

MOON
swoon, loon, bassoon, tune, croon, June, prune, Neptune, over so soon?

UNDEAD
foldout bed, in the head, often misread, heavily bled, that's what *she* said!

⊬ how to celebrate the holidays with your vampire ⊬

He'll take the holy right out of "holiday," so let's call them *feast days* since he's probably used to celebrating by filling up on fresh blood. (Your family probably won't appreciate him painting lamb's blood over your door on Passover just so he can lick it off when you've gone to bed.) Here's how to celebrate with the undead man of your dreams!

❄ new year's eve

Don't "ring" in the new year—the shrill sounds will leave you kissing the breeze at midnight while he silently broods in the nearest graveyard. We recommend not doing anything special for this one. It's just a reminder of how old he is, and he's likely to be moodier than usual.

❄ st. george's day

In some countries, this Christian feast day marks the first time sheep were driven from pasture for the season. Oh, and all the evil in the world is supposedly free to sweep through the land at the stroke of midnight. No matter—make it a romantic affair! Take a late-night buggy ride out to the country and picnic under the foggy skies—he'll love the fresh lamb's blood!

❄ winter solstice

What better alternative to Christmas and the Festival of Lights?! Put away those nativity sets and toss the dreidels out with the latkes in order to celebrate the longest night of the year. You'll be up all night reveling in the glory of darkness and gloom.

❊ all hallow's eve

The spirits are heading out of their sepulchers and his dead family and friends are sure to join your soiree. They probably won't eat much, so decor should be the focus. Since you probably already have a vampire-friendly establishment, add some extra-special touches like a few cobwebs and a touch of fog—your guests will feel right at home. Try some Halloween party games to entertain! Bob for apples—fangs really come in handy here—play pin the scythe on the Reaper, and take a swing at a Van Helsing piñata.

by now, you've surely realized that anything you can do, a vampire can do much, much better, whether it's writing poems, bobbing for apples, or looking aloof and fabulous. You will always be the meat loaf to his filet mignon, the generic toilet paper to his Charmin, the Mandy Moore to his Kelly Clarkson. However, there's one activity at which humans far surpass their immortal brethren: crafts. Make sure to show your vampire your artistic side. He'll be less inclined to trade you in for an upgrade if he knows you'll make his coffin all comfy cozy.

Don't panic—there are plenty of crafts that won't take too much time away from letting him watch you sleep or getting yourself into perilous situations. Weaving your own fabric might be hard unless you live in Amish country. Even knitting him a sweater would take too long. But a quick trip to the craft store can get you some embroidery floss, aida fabric, and embroidery needles, and then you're all set to make him a sweet cross-stitch. Bonus: Let him admire your graceful hands while you're sewing, and you might get a villanelle about your delicate knuckles!

vampire cross-stitch

Here's the one cross that won't turn him into dust—a cross-stitch! Use two strands of embroidery floss to thread the needle—in the chart, X means to make a full cross-stitch, and / means to make only the first half, from the bottom left of the stitch to the top right.

Whether he is near or far, into poetry or into crafts, there's no guarantee that your vampire will remain interested. If you really think his moon is starting to wane, you might have to resort to more extreme measures.

My vampire boyfriend loves to save me—it's one of his biggest turn-ons. Whenever I feel like he's getting a little bored with the relationship, I like to stumble and fall in front of an 18-wheeler and let him save me. Works like a charm every time.

—LUCY, 16

I hadn't been to church in about five years. I called my grandmother and told her I wanted to go to Saturday night Mass with her. She nearly fainted, but that's a whole other conversation. My point is, it totally drove my vampire crazy. He was all like, "But you can't do this to me!" and I was all like, "Yeah, I know, but I need to explore my options." (Like, how good was that line?!) The whole time I was at Mass, I could see him circling the church, throwing shadows across all the stained-glass windows. It was so romantic! And he *totally* wanted me after that, if you get my meaning. I highly recommend getting in touch with your religious side to drive him wild.

—REESE, 15

Setting aside time for yourself

Nothing says "I matter" like remembering to take some time out for yourself. After all, if you aren't refreshed, relaxed, and *robust*, how do you expect your vampire to see that you are obviously the girl of his undead dreams? No one likes a Debbie Downer, so spend some important one-on-one time with that special someone — you! Don't forget that absence (in very small doses) can make his icy heart grow fonder. Take some time for yourself and he'll be even more ecstatic to see you the next day!

✳ unwind

All those late nights making you feel like a paranoid delusional? Unwind with some herbal tea (no caffeine needed!), soft music, and a popular vampire book. You'll be slumbering in less than two minutes flat, attracting a certain someone to your window, so plan ahead. No frumpy pajamas for you!

✳ play

After months of careful planning, plotting, and primping, here's your chance to put that spring back in your step by getting outside and being spontaneous! Of course, don't be *too* spontaneous. Apply ample amounts of sunscreen, wear clothing that keeps every square inch of your body covered, throw on that wide-brimmed hat for extra coverage, and don't forget your sunglasses! Now get out there!

❋ See your friends

Remember those people you used to hang out with? Maybe you passed them notes during class, or sat with them during lunch, or got together each weekend for coffee. They're probably all still around, wondering where you've been lately. Time to return some phone calls and check their online statuses. You've probably found some stores with great vintage corsets—maybe your best friend (whatever her name was) would like to go shopping with you.

❋ Have a "you" night

Dating a vampire can wear out a girl. He's a perfect specimen of physical perfection, but mortals have to work hard to be so perfectly groomed. And if he's seeing you every night, you're under pressure to look perfect all the time. Take a night off! Close the blinds in case he's watching from outside and take a long, hot bath. Give yourself a pedicure, and paint your toenails a different color than your fingernails. Mash an avocado into a face mask without worrying about him seeing you looking green. Read some of those magazines he hates, or crack open an Anne Rice novel where he won't see you reading it. Light the scented candles that are too strong for his superhuman sense of smell, and lounge in your comfiest pajamas—it's okay if they're the ugliest, too!

❋ Do the things you can't do when he's around

Gargle with some holy water—you won't be kissing him tonight! That cross necklace? Wear it! Garlic on your pizza? Go for it. Take off all your Band-Aids and air those scrapes out. Pull up your shades and let the sunlight in. Revel in your mortality—while it lasts.

relationship affirmations

Dating a vampire can be tough. But chin up, human! Try these affirmations for quelling the difficult feelings you might have during your relationship.

overwhelmed by general inadequacy

I am only a puny mortal. He can't expect too much of me.
I am only a puny mortal. He can't expect too much of me.

catching his roving eye

I *might* have a week before he dumps me!
I *might* have a week before he dumps me!

worried he might kill you

My blood is probably yucky!
My blood is probably yucky!

Once you've been dating long enough, the question of eternity is bound to come up. How lucky for you, then, that it also comes up in the next chapter!

is your burning an eternal flame?

ternity . . . it's a long time. Believe me, I know. You mortals have it easy. When you say, "Till death do us part," you're talking a hundred years, max. Vampires can wait that long for a dentist's appointment—a century is nothing to us. When you say you want to be with a vampire always and forever, you mean . . . always and forever. The only way for this to happen is for him to give you that (un)deadly bite you've been waiting for. But first, you must weigh the pros and cons of switching to the immortality track.

pros and cons of becoming a vampire

pros

You'll live to find out whether the future ends up looking like **the world in WALL-E.**

You don't have to be nice to people you don't like. Hissing is encouraged!

Naturally minty-fresh breath. Think of all the money you'll save on Listerine.

Guaranteed straight A's by the time you start high school for the fifth time.

You'll be the hottest girl in school (including Caitlin and her totally fake new nose).

Even if you're the hottest girl in school, **Caitlin won't be alive to be jealous of you.**

Watching all the endangered animals go extinct. Could you really live in a world without the Philippine warty pig? No, I thought not.

Barry Manilow night on *American Idol* is going to get really old by season 214.

Remember how sick you got of Jell-O when you got your wisdom teeth taken out? Now imagine **drinking nothing but blood for 3,000 years.** It doesn't even come in "berry blue."

High School Musical 81.

cons

are you ready to become a vampire?

1. **How close are you and your vampire boyfriend?**
   a. He spends every night writing sonnets about the starlight reflecting off your eyelids.
   b. Things are okay—it's not your fault you don't understand what he means when he starts speaking in Middle English—which he does all the time.
   c. Super-close! He loves you, and so does his family. You think it's cute that his little brother has a crush on you, even though he sort of wants to drink your blood.

2. **During the week, how many nights will your vampire spend gazing through your window?**
   a. Every night—unless he comes inside and you sleep in his cold arms.
   b. You only notice him there a couple times a week.
   c. Every night—unless he's off somewhere, hunting less adorable victims.

3. **What bothers you the most about your relationship?**
   a. The blood-drinking, the Transylvanian accent, the brooding, the fact that you can't go to the beach with your friends. . . .
   b. It's hard that he's nocturnal—you're spending all your money on Red Bull.
   c. It's terrible that you have to sleep, and go to school, and eat, and pretend to have a normal life—you just want to be with your vampire all the time!

4. What's your plan for the next several years?

   a. Becoming undead and staying with your boyfriend . . . forever.

   b. Chilling with your vampire boyfriend, going on midnight walks, and trying not to fall prey to evil vampires who want to kill you.

   c. Graduating from high school, going to college, and working in the local ice-cream parlor this summer.

5. What would be the worst thing about being undead?

   a. That whole drinking blood thing is a little icky.

   b. Nothing your boyfriend does could be bad—vampires are beautiful and unspeakably romantic!

   c. Not being able to look in the mirror, not being able to go out in the sun, drinking blood, being compelled to write poetry all the time . . . the list goes on and on.

6. Why do you want to be a vampire?

   a. You're beginning to wonder that yourself. Drinking blood and killing people sort of negates the cooler aspects.

   b. Everything! Perfect skin, awesome clothes, charming old castles, and being with your boyfriend for eternity!

   c. Being able to run ridiculously fast and jump really high would be kinda cool.

7. Have you ever: (check all that apply)

   __ Wished your rare steak was just a little less cooked?

   __ Hissed when something startled you?

   __ Gotten thirsty at a blood drive?

   __ Gone for long walks through the cemetery at night, even when your vampire boyfriend was away?

   __ Wished your bed had walls and a lid?

__ Tried on red-colored contacts and thought you looked pretty hot?
__ Found yourself obsessing over your dental hygiene?
__ Stayed up all night?
__ Peeled a blood orange and been disappointed when it was just fruit?
__ Stayed inside on days when it's just too sunny out?

Scoring

GIVE YOURSELF THE FOLLOWING POINTS FOR EACH ANSWER.

1. **a.** 1 **b.** 0 **c.** 2
2. **a.** 2 **b.** 0 **c.** 1
3. **a.** 0 **b.** 1 **c.** 2
4. **a.** 2 **b.** 1 **c.** 0
5. **a.** 1 **b.** 2 **c.** 0
6. **a.** 0 **b.** 2 **c.** 1
7. Give yourself 1 point for every statement you checked.

FOR A SCORE OF 0 TO 7 POINTS

Are you sure you should even be dating a vampire? Really, you should be flattered that your vampire boyfriend was even willing to take a chance on a girl with a tan! You're nowhere close to vampire material.

FOR A SCORE OF 8 TO 14 POINTS

Not undead yet. It sounds like you're overcome by your boyfriend's hotness but aren't quite ready to become a vampire yourself.

FOR A SCORE OF 15 TO 22 POINTS

Are you sure you're not a vampire already? Next time you're making out with your boyfriend, offer him your neck and hope he doesn't accidentally drain your veins!

Do I want to keep Mandy around? I go back and forth on that one. On one hand, the thought of being with her until time ends is . . . daunting, to say the least. On the other hand, it's really creeping me out to watch her aging.

—ALARIC, 223

I'm going to be honest: You think you want to be with her forever, and then the moment you do it, you're like, "Oh sweet mother of vampires, what have I done?" There's a moment of biter's remorse, and that moment lasts a long, long time.

—GREGOR, 498

I've never found "the one." Don't get me wrong—I've met a lot of great human girls. Some have been girlfriends, some have been snacks. Hundreds of them have really, really touched me. But one girl for all eternity? Let's just say that's a long time to share a coffin.

—GUSTAVO, 182

Six ways to hint that you're ready for eternity

So, yes, your vampire might need a little convincing. Just because you're ready to spend eternity as his vampire life partner/super-hot undead paramour, it doesn't mean that he's about to commit till "wooden stakes do you part." He may not even know that you're prepared to take that leap because, although your vampire is probably near perfect, he's not psychic. (Okay, you're right, he might be *psychic*, but when it comes to matters of eternity, he may choose to turn a blind third eye.) Here are some ways to introduce the subject without scaring him off.

1 ❄ **SURPRISE HIM WITH TICKETS** for the Winter Olympics . . . in 2332.

2 ❄ **GIVE HIM A SAGUARO CACTUS** (the world's slowest-growing plant) for Valentine's Day. In the card, tell him how you look forward to watching your love blossom like the cactus's flowers. (The first should appear in about sixteen years.)

3 ❄ **ON YOUR NEXT ROMANTIC NIGHTTIME STROLL,** gaze up at the sky and tell him that you're excited to live in a moon colony someday, after they work out the kinks.

4 ❄ **PASS ON A CHANCE TO GO SNOWBOARDING** while you're still "breakable." It'll be much more fun when you're indestructible and won't have to wear ugly goggles.

5 ❄ **REFUSE TO APOLOGIZE** for forgetting your best friend's birthday because "she'll be dead in eighty years anyway."

6 ❄ **CHANGE YOUR ONLINE RELATIONSHIP STATUS** to "eternally linked" and see if he confirms.

before making such a big decision, it's important to ask people you trust to evaluate your motives and your sanity. If they say go for it, then go for it! And if they seem hesitant, just assume they're part of the great anti-vampire conspiracy and find someone else (like me) to ask.

After five years together, we were getting pretty serious. One night, while we were strolling through the dark woods behind my house, he leaned in, lifted the hair off my neck, and bit me—right in the jugular. It was spine-tinglingly romantic!

Now we've been together for seventy-five years and the only reason he hasn't left me is because he feels guilty about turning me into a vampire. Eternity is not all it's cracked up to be. It gives you time to discover all his really annoying habits, like taking up the whole coffin, leaving bloodstains on our best dining linens, and eyeing the zombie next door. Sometimes, I just wish I were dead. Seriously.

—EUGENIA, 90

My daughter, Olivia, begged her creepy undead boyfriend to take her away from her "painfully dull" life with us. I told her that if she planned to stay with him, she shouldn't bother to come home. Obviously, she's got bats in her belfry . . . and probably her living room.

It's been twenty-two years since I've seen them. He probably left her for a werewolf or something. I warned her that eternity was a long time. If they are still together, they're probably hanging from the dirty roof of a cave somewhere.

—SUSIE, AGE UNDISCLOSED

*O*h, *Vlad!* you're exclaiming in a way that is not entirely becoming of you. *I'm ready. Take me, you well-coiffed source of my undoing! Take me!*

I would splash cold water on your face if I weren't afraid that the pages you are holding would get wet. You're all ready to turn yourself over to him (or, in this case, me), aren't you?

Well, not so fast. Because while you might think the path to forever is only two small bite marks away, you are probably ignoring a crucial fact: The vampire is just not that into you.

Seriously, he's not.

Want to know why? Turn to part three.

A NOTE FROM GRETA, A VAMPIRE SLAYER

DEAR WANNABE VAMPIRE,

AWW, YOU GUYS ARE PLANNING TO ~~GROW OLD~~ STAY FOREVER YOUNG TOGETHER. HOW UTTERLY CUTE! YOU BOTH MUST BE SO EXCITED TO DO THINGS LIKE SURPRISE EACH OTHER WITH A FRESH, FOURTEEN-YEAR-OLD CATCH OF THE DAY FOR DINNER. I ENVY YOU SO. ALMOST.

DO YOU REALLY GET WHAT "PERMANENT" MEANS? IF YOU CHANGE YOUR MIND, YOU DON'T GET TO CLICK YOUR DOC MARTENS AND SAY, "THERE'S NO FLESH LIKE HUMANS'" THREE TIMES TO SWITCH BACK. YOUR HORMONALLY CHARGED TEENAGE HEART HAS TROUBLE DECIDING WHAT TO WEAR TO A DRIVER'S ED CLASS — HOW DO YOU EXPECT TO MAKE THIS (LITERALLY) LIFE-CHANGING DECISION?

IF YOU DECIDE TO IGNORE MY ADVICE. I'M AFRAID THERE ARE ONLY TWO OPTIONS LEFT. ONE, YOU'RE TOMORROW NIGHT'S DINNER. TWO, YOU ACTUALLY SURVIVE TELLING YOUR BOYFRIEND YOU WANT TO BE A VAMPIRE AND HE GIVES YOU A BITE TO REMEMBER. SO NOW YOU'RE REALLY, TRULY A VAMPIRE? CONGRATULATIONS! YOU'RE NEXT ON MY LIST.

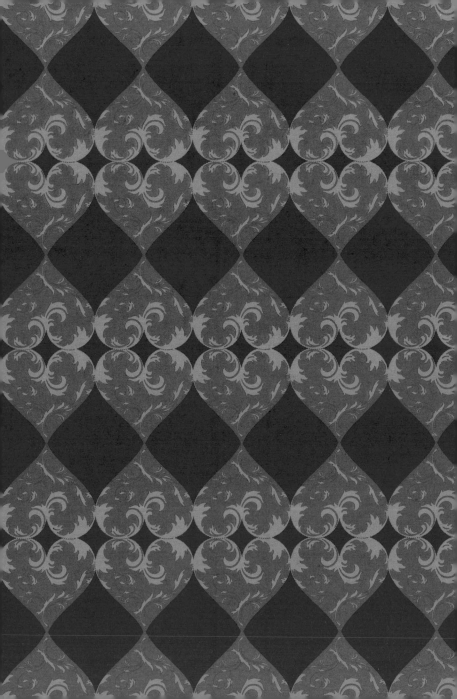

✦

the vampire is just not that into you

it's not him, it's you

Y ou thought it was going so well! You thought he was yours, all yours! When he pledged eternal devotion, you believed him! This is completely understandable—you're only human, after all.

What your mortal eyes can't see is that he's getting restless. Blood always smells sweeter when it's hard to get. He's used to you now, and familiarity breeds a desire not to breed. Maybe your human vulnerability and weakness were cute at first. But it's no match for a vampire's cold, hard . . . intellect.

In his mind it's clear: The problem isn't him. It's you.

eight things he can't stand about you

1 ✴ You eat three meals a day, shoveling chemically treated products into your mouth nonstop. Nauseating.

2 ✴ You bathe regularly.

3 ✴ You talk about which college you have to get into. He's already been through this seventeen times.

4 ✴ You keep asking him about his feelings. They really don't vary that much.

5 ✴ You make him the photographer when you and your friends hang out. Just because he won't appear in the pictures doesn't mean he wants to take them for you.

6 ✴ You don't know the difference between Schubert and Beethoven, but you can identify each Jonas Brother by his eyebrow shape.

7 ✴ You call him during daylight hours. Some people are trying to sleep.

8 ✴ Your body is way too warm. It's like cuddling up to a baked fish.

Admittedly, it can be difficult to determine whether your vampire is losing interest — we vampires are hardly forthright with our emotions. The signs aren't always consistent. Sometimes, an impromptu trip to Italy and a hastily scribbled *I love you so much that I can never see you again— good-bye forever* really means *See you in a few days.* Other times, it means *It's over. No, seriously. Give me back my Transylvania High varsity jacket. My new girlfriend is cold.*

If you're unsure, I've compiled some data on key vampire behaviors for your education. The numbers never lie.

decoding what he does when he's around you

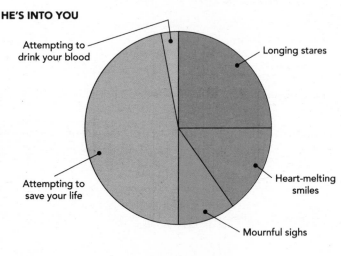

HE'S INTO YOU

- Attempting to drink your blood
- Longing stares
- Attempting to save your life
- Heart-melting smiles
- Mournful sighs

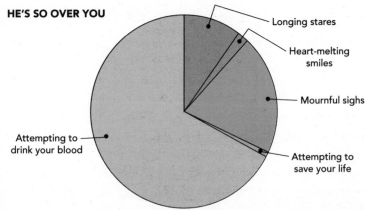

HE'S SO OVER YOU

- Longing stares
- Heart-melting smiles
- Mournful sighs
- Attempting to drink your blood
- Attempting to save your life

TYPICAL RELATIONSHIP TRAJECTORY

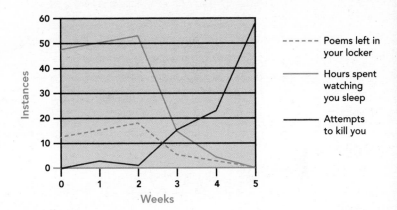

- - - - - Poems left in your locker

——— Hours spent watching you sleep

——— Attempts to kill you

AVERAGE RELATIONSHIP LENGTH BASED ON GIRLFRIEND TYPE

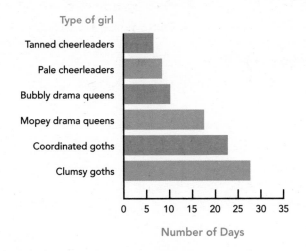

hints he may not be that into you

Because he does not want to hurt your tender feelings, the hints he's dropping might not be the portrait of obviousness that most human boys paint when they want to get out of a relationship. Instead of reading between the lines (which is, let's face it, only blank space), try reading *underneath* them.

HE SAYS: "I'm going hunting."

HE MEANS: "Puny mortal, you are beginning to bore me."

HE SAYS: "I need space."

HE MEANS: "One hundred years ought to do it."

HE SAYS: "I love you too much to change you into a monster like me."

HE MEANS: "There is *no way* I'm keeping you for eternity."

HE SAYS: "I searched eternity for you."

HE MEANS: "I've dated a lot. And yeah, they were hot. Get over it."

HE SAYS: "You *must* go to college, my little human pet."

HE MEANS: "Go to school across the country, if possible."

HE SAYS: "Promise me you'll stay safe."

HE MEANS: "Honestly, it's pretty annoying that you always need saving when I'm in the middle of watching *Dexter*."

is he tired of you?

Do you still refuse to believe me that it's over? Will you only be happy if you discover it in quiz form? Fine. Be that way. Such stubbornness is probably one of the reasons his mind is starting to wander back to the grave.

1. **You send him a text message saying, "I nicked my leg shaving and it won't stop bleeding!" How does he respond?**
   a. "That's too bad. Get a Band-Aid."
   b. He doesn't respond.
   c. "Did you hit an artery?"
   d. He shows up at your door with roses and a goblet.

2. **His latest poem to you was titled:**
   a. "Hemoglobin Halitosis: You Have It"
   b. "High Noon"
   c. "I Can't Take It Anymore!"
   d. "Fangs of Smoldering Emotion"

3. **You wear a turtleneck on your next date to see how your vampire reacts. What happens?**
   a. He stands you up! Did he see you standing there and walk in the other direction?
   b. Five minutes into the date he claims his stomach is upset from something he ate and goes home.
   c. When you head back from the ladies' room, you find him carving the waitress's phone number into his arm.
   d. He looks disappointed and asks why you covered up such a "divine neck."

4. **You're at the blood bank donating some plasma. As you're conversing with your vampire, a drop-dead gorgeous goth girl walks by, a small trickle of blood escaping from under the Band-Aid on her arm. What does he do?**
   a. He pretends not to notice her, even though he so does.
   b. He forgets what he was saying as his smoldering eyes track her every move.
   c. He gets up and says he'll be right back as he follows the girl out the door.
   d. He looks you in the eyes and tells you how beautiful you are.

5. **Getting desperate, you decide to ignite his passions by letting him save you from death. While walking along train tracks under a full moon, you stumble and fall as a train is approaching. How does your vampire react?**
   a. He sighs, rolls his eyes, and pulls you out of the way.
   b. He stands there and says, "Okay, you should get up now."
   c. He ties you to the tracks.
   d. He makes a dramatic show of plucking you from danger's way. Once safe, he cradles you in his strong arms and calls you his "precious."

⊹⊱ Scoring ⊰⊹

✤ **IF YOU ANSWERED MOSTLY A's:** He's getting tired of you.
✤ **IF YOU ANSWERED MOSTLY B's:** He's really getting tired of you.
✤ **IF YOU ANSWERED MOSTLY C's:** He pretty much hates you.
✤ **IF YOU ANSWERED D's AND ONLY D's:** He's still into you.

The girlfriend I had last century had this idea that I'd turn her into a vampire and that we would stay happily together for the rest of eternity. This was after we'd been dating only for six months or so. I'm much too young for that sort of commitment, but when I tried to tell her so, she started snapping at anyone who spoke to her. The vampire is supposed to be the moody, brooding one in the relationship! I determined it better to end things rather than try to deal with such juvenile behavior, so I bit her...and not in the eternal sense.

—TRISTRAM, 346

You wonder why guys are always busy when they're losing interest? It's because we are. Cleaning the crypt, flossing, organizing taxidermy collections—all more fun than being with a girl we're tired of. Sorry!

—CHARLES, 803

The tracker wanted her. I said go ahead. Now the tracker and I have been together for ninety-eight years!

—BERTRAND, 302

Because he's dead on the outside, it's sometimes hard to tell that he's dying on the inside. But the fact that you are so oblivious isn't helping matters any.

I haven't seen Gustavo in two years now. Well, two years, four months, twelve days, and three hours. But it's *totally* because my blood smelled too good and he was worried about being able to restrain himself. I know one day he'll come back and we'll be together again, me on his cold lap in my ski hat and long johns, him with his fangs nuzzling lovingly against my neck. Just the way it used to be. I just hope he comes back before I'm old and wrinkly. Or, you know, before senior prom.

—JENNA, 17

After Elijah canceled our date for the third night in a row, I stopped by my friend Melissa's house to get some advice. I thought it was weird that Elijah's car was parked outside so I climbed into the tree by her bedroom window. That's when I discovered he was cheating on me with that skanky vampire baiter! I was so shocked that I fell out of the tree. Elijah didn't even try to save me. That's when I knew things were over.

—MARIE, 17

Over the many, many, many years I have been alive, I have racked up an incredible number of degrees from universities around the world. I have not, however, dabbled in the psychotherapeutic arts. So I would like to refer you to one of my colleagues, Dr. Thaddeus Phillips, who has done extensive research in this field and received a VD (Vampire Doctorate) from Fangsylvania University in the former Soviet Union.

FROM THE DESK OF DR. THADDEUS PHILLIPS, VD

I can sense the fear in your union. It is fear that translates into the emotional pain you inevitably feel in this unconventional relationship and the literal pain that is pending if you continue down this path of whining all the time. He may be the bloodsucker, but you, my friend, are the leech. If you continue to stalk him when he should be stalking you, how will he express his love? Trust yourself to trust him to trust you to trust him. It's simple, really.

I also encourage you to be one with silence and reduce your whining, particularly because his ears are not accustomed to the decibels you reach. While he is young in appearance, he is clearly aged in tolerance, particularly for you.

Ultimately, you mustn't point out what is lacking in him, but what is lacking in your inadequate blood. Be honest with yourself about the real predator in the relationship — it's you, not him.

— Dr. Thaddeus Phillips, VD, Esteemed Expert on Special Relationships

what to do when your relationship has one foot in the grave

My little mortal flower, your days are numbered. Wait! I must clarify—*your* days have always been numbered, but your relationship is dying, too. It has one foot in the grave—and not in the right direction, either. Try to stave off the inevitable with these last-ditch efforts.

❋ make him jealous

Vampires have a reputation for being possessive, but it would never occur to us that you could be attracted by another. Your best bet? Try flirting with a werewolf. Just make sure you don't get bitten. Because if you start getting all hairy, the relationship is *really* over.

❋ more "accidents"

You had a range of near-death experiences in the courting phase. He's saved you from traffic collisions, thug attacks, and overexposure in the woods. Let's face it—he's a little bored. Inject a syringe of adrenaline in the vein of your relationship by adding variety to your "accidents." Shark attacks are always fun, and plane crashes have a *je ne sais quoi* he'll enjoy. Avoid rare diseases. He can't save you, and there's no way he's going to visit you in the hospital.

❋ the brush-off

It's bold. It's sneaky. It's kind of devilish in its brilliance. Try breaking up with *him* before he dumps you! It will be the first time it's ever happened to him, and it might just shock him into being interested again.

✳ clinging

You can't *really* cling to him. He has houses all over the world, and he can fly, after all. But hey — if it makes you feel better to humiliate yourself by calling and begging, who am I to stop you?

✳ pretend you've already been changed

You've begged him to change you and he's said no. You sense him pulling away, and your desperation is mounting. Here's an idea for you — trick him into thinking he's changed you into a vampire already! Vampires have been known to get absentminded when bloodlust is upon them, so here's how to pull it off:

1. Slaughter a pig outside his crypt to distract him.
2. Smear on white pancake makeup.
3. Put in red contacts.
4. Say things like, *Time has no meaning for me now*, and *I never noticed that the world is dying*.
5. Regularly plunge yourself into ice-water baths.

don't want to be the blood rain on your passion parade, but if I'm not going to be honest with you, who will be? Certainly not your vampire. As a policy, honesty ranks up there with dog-petting and sunbathing for him. He's not going to be directly truthful with you — which means you have to start being directly truthful with yourself. As you'll see in the next chapter, you may discover a few things about yourself that you didn't want to know.

it's not you, it's him

In the interest of fairness and balance, I must share with you now a little from Dr. Thaddeus Phillips's fifty-seventh ex-wife, Jane. While Jane, a human, does not have the same VD (Vampire Doctorate) as her ex-husband, she has also studied human–vampire romance extensively, and has drawn some different conclusions than the esteemed Dr. Phillips.

While I realize that Dr. Oakes is referring to other vampires and not yours truly, I still must take exception to her aspersions. I do lots of things to keep my love life interesting. Like, write books! Which I will eventually get around to giving to my love, Sarah, to read. I mean, Abby. I mean — what year is it? — Felicia.

Okay, fine. Sometimes we get bored. But not all of us are *cheaters*.

is he seeing someone (or something) else?

1. **You're playing with his cell phone when he gets a strange text message—what does it say?**
   a. Hey, still on 4 baseball?
   b. Sry bout last nite, my pack hates the undead.
   c. R we getting 2gether 2nite 4 a movie?
   d. I'm in the woods...alone and vulnerable....
   e. Great talking 2 u yesterday—I <3 a guy with brains.

2. **He's lounging gracefully on your bed, reading Tennyson, when he suddenly has to leave. What's his excuse?**
   a. "Promised my mom I'd run an errand for her before midnight!"
   b. "Full moon—gotta run."
   c. "Just wanted to spend the night in the crypt."
   d. "There's something I wanted to watch tonight."
   e. "Getting some dinner, or might be dinner? It could be an interesting role reversal."

3. **You're in his tomb and notice a book open on his nightstand—what is it?**
   a. *How to Cook Everything Vegetarian* by Mark Bittman
   b. *Shiver* by Maggie Stiefvater
   c. *Blue Bloods* by Melissa de la Cruz
   d. *Breaking Dawn* by Stephenie Meyer
   e. *Zombie Blondes* by Brian James

4. **You notice his interests have changed lately. All of a sudden he:**
   a. Has started sitting in a different tree near your window.
   b. Says he wants a puppy.
   c. Seems colder than ever, and more bloodthirsty.
   d. No longer notices when you wear a scarf.
   e. Is really into horror movies, like *28 Days Later*.

5. **You call his castle, but he's not home. His mom says he's:**
   a. Playing baseball with his little brother.
   b. In the Black Forest—and took a silver sword with him, "just in case."
   c. In Transylvania with an old ~~flame~~ friend.
   d. On a rescue mission.
   e. Doing something that required him to take a helmet when he left.

6. **His journal was open and you didn't mean to look! But you still saw that he had written:**
   a. In the middle of poem—stuck on good rhyme for "nostril."
   b. Went running—she needed four legs to keep up with me!
   c. Best. Blood bank. Date. Ever!
   d. I just love the scent of new blood.
   e. I feel like she might just be after me for my brains.

Scoring

❄ IF YOU ANSWERED MOSTLY A's

Silly! Everyone has family obligations, and he's no exception. Stop reading his journal and emails already! Nothing kills a vampire's ardor faster than a jealous girlfriend.

✳ IF YOU ANSWERED MOSTLY B's

It sounds like his new romantic interest needs to do more than just shave her legs to look presentable for a vampire — your competition is probably furry, changes according to the moon, runs on four legs, and acts pretty canine. He doesn't want a puppy, he wants a girl werewolf!

✳ IF YOU ANSWERED MOSTLY C's

Nice knowing you! Your boyfriend is flirting with another vampire, and there's not a whole lot you can do. They both want the same things out of life (or, rather, death): blood, dark creepy castles, and blood. You can try driving a stake through her heart, but if you miss, you better run for your life!

✳ IF YOU ANSWERED MOSTLY D's

Your vampire is craving a certain blood type — and it isn't yours! It sounds like your boyfriend is seeing another human. And don't even think about exacting revenge on the hussy, because your vampire will be protecting her. Try breaking up with him and making him jealous by going out with a werewolf.

✳ IF YOU ANSWERED MOSTLY E's

His new girl is out for one thing and one thing only: BRRRAAAAAIIINS! That's right, he's got a zombie after him. It's hard to understand the attraction — that vacant expression, the decaying flesh, the stiff walk, and awful hair. Maybe he likes that they can get one human for lunch and split it — he gets the blood, she gets the brains. Unless you can get in a direct shot to the head, there's not much you can do to get rid of this one. Try to take comfort in the fact that she's probably only trying to get into his skull — hopefully he'll come to his senses and come back to you.

vampire zodiac chart

Even though their bright presence can ruin a perfectly good black night, you might try to consult the stars to see if your relationship can be saved. Fair enough. But be warned—when it comes to the zodiac, humans are easy to predict . . . but vampires are off the chart.

---

aries ✳ *(March 21–April 19)* **Key traits:** Bold, passionate, pioneering

What attracts you to vampires: Your fiery personality.

The bad news: Vampires are used to being the leaders in a relationship, and don't follow well. Not a good match.

---

taurus ✳ *(April 20–May 20)* **Key traits:** Persistent, devoted, stable

What attracts you to vampires: He's in need of direction, and your domineering nature meshes well with his.

The bad news: Vampires aren't stable enough and will mock your craving for security. Not a good match.

---

gemini ✳ *(May 21–June 20)* **Key traits:** Social, witty, lively

What attracts you to vampires: Your innate curiosity.

The bad news: Your cunning makes vampires nervous, and they don't like being nervous. Not a good match.

---

cancer ✳ *(June 21–July 22)* **Key traits:** Intuitive, emotional, sensitive

What attracts you to vampires: Your sympathetic nature draws you to anyone in need—and he needs you.

The bad news: You're too moody, and vampires like to be the brooding ones in a relationship. Not a good match.

leo ✳ *(July 23–August 22)*

Key traits: Lively, attention-seeking, theatrical

What attracts you to vampires: You want to inject some of your sunny personality into his aged soul.

The bad news: Leo is sunny and warm, and vampires can't tolerate the sun. Not a good match.

---

virgo ✳ *(August 23–September 22)*

Key traits: Shy, meticulous, modest

What attracts you to vampires: You know a vampire will protect you from the world.

The bad news: Vampires are always going to be bigger perfectionists than you are. Not a good match.

---

libra ✳ *(September 23–October 23)*

Key traits: Diplomatic, sociable, open-minded

What attracts you to vampires: You're interested in dating people from all species.

The bad news: Vampires hate it when you flirt with other undead, and you just can't help yourself. Not a good match.

---

scorpio ✳ *(October 24–November 22)*

Key traits: Exciting, obsessive, untamable

What attracts you to vampires: You're as tempestuous and stormy as he is.

The bad news: Vampires are jealous, but they hate it when you become possessive. Not a good match.

$agittarius$  *(November 23–December 21)*

Key traits: Jovial, philosophical, positive

What attracts you to vampires: You're excited by the musings of the undead.

The bad news: Vampires are cynical, and think you're too blindly optimistic. Not a good match.

---

capricorn *(December 22–January 19)*

Key traits: Patient, prudent, reserved

What attracts you to vampires: You like to make sense out of nonsensical unions.

The bad news: Vampires don't like grudges, and they can hold them for centuries longer than you can. Not a good match.

---

aquarius *(January 20–February 19)*

Key traits: Progressive, unemotional, humanitarian

What attracts you to vampires: You're always eager to give everyone a chance—human or not.

The bad news: A vampire's cold heart will leave even detached Aquarius emotionally drained. Not a good match.

---

pisces *(February 20–March 20)*

Key traits: Sensitive, idealistic, escapist

What attracts you to vampires: You're already imagining eternity with him.

The bad news: Vampires will mistake your sensitivity for weakness, and they despise weakness. Not a good match.

I thought it was a little...*strange*, let's say, when Charles started encouraging me to pursue my dream of becoming a water-skiing performer (you know, like at SeaWorld? That's gonna be me!). Before, he was all like, "But, darling, that's so bright an ambition." He couldn't stand my being outdoors so often. Then, just when I thought it was going so well, he was all, "You're starting to look a bit too pale, don't you think?" and "I hear it's going to be sunny and eighty degrees today!" and "Don't you think you're better suited to someone like Josh Aberdeen?" Which, duh, of course I am—Josh is a water-skiing *god*. Then, next thing I know, there's a box on my doorstep tied with a beautiful black ribbon and inside, a sequined leotard and feathered headpiece. I knew it was over. How cruel can you get?

—ABIGAIL, 16

You need to show some pride here. If his heart is out the door, you had better leave the room before his restraint does. You've always loved his killer smile, but you've never wanted it to be *that* killer. Keep watch for the signs that's it's time to go.

ten signs it's time to leave him

1 ❄ His pet name for you changes from "Darling Angel Sweet Pea" to "Snack Pack."

2 ❄ He creates a profile for you on an online dating site.

3 ❄ You call him because there's a tracker outside your house and he tells you, "Yeah, sorry about that."

10 ❄ His love poems start to suck. Rhyming "you should find a human" with "someone whose blood's really zoomin'"? Not a good sign.

4 ❄ He returns the tickets you gave him for the 2332 Olympics because he says he thinks he's busy that day.

9 ❄ He encourages you to apply to foreign colleges and assures you that you'll have an "amazing time" in Yemen.

5 ❄ Instead of carrying you to your car on icy days, he gives you a pair of hiking boots and advises you to "start practicing."

8 ❄ When you ask why he no longer guards your room every night, he says your snoring is enough to make the Volturi rip their own heads off.

7 ❄ You cut your finger and he admonishes you for being wasteful.

6 ❄ He asks that you stop talking about his glorious, minty breath . . . . It's just creepy.

If you think regular human guys are hard to read, try dating a vampire. It's hard to tell if he's just grown a little more emo than usual, or if he wants to bury our relationship in the catacombs. My ex-boyfriend started staying in on weekends, complaining that it was too bright to go outside—even at night. (We live in Oregon—not exactly the land of the midnight sun.) And he kept coming up with dumb excuses to keep me from coming over, too—like he had a cold or tuberculosis or something. I'm pretty sure undead people can't actually get sick. Then I caught him out at a baseball game on a Friday night...with a banshee. Game o-v-e-r.

—WILLA, 18

It's really weird. Alaric dragged me deep into the woods and said I should forget all about him. When I walked all the way back home, I found that all my photos of him were gone, and so were all the presents he gave me. The fifty volumes of poetry he wrote about my beauty, the gown he gave me for the monsters' ball, the special armored car—everything! He has totally disappeared, and his family left town, too. Is this, like, another vampire game? I know he's trying to tell me something, but *what*?

—MANDY, 15

who hasn't been in a relationship where all the things you used to love are suddenly becoming annoying? The whole idea of him sucking blood used to be a turn-on . . . but now you've had enough of his blood breath. (Especially *morning* blood breath—ew.) Moonlit walks were romantic at first . . . now they're just annoying. After all, a girl's gotta sleep!

You were fine hanging out with his buddies at the crypt. Really, you were. But how many conversations can one group of friends have about the Vampire World Series? And yes, at first wearing black gave him attitude. Now you realize it's merely a lack of fashion sense.

He's out of touch when it comes to music, movies, and hygiene. Yes, he'll fly you around at night—but it gets cold up there! Not that he would know. In fact, there are lots of things he'll never know about. He says he won't read your mind, but maybe he should read your lips some of the time.

You've begun to suspect that maybe he's just been after your blood all along. You've seen pictures of his exes . . . on milk cartons. His nicknames for you are all food-related. ("Honey" or "Cupcake" are acceptable. But "Breakfast," "Lunch," and "Dinner" are not. "Sweetheart" is deeply ambiguous.) He avoids the mall and school dances, and he schedules all your dates in desolate places such as rock quarries and out-of-the-way railroad crossings. And when he does manage to take you out to dinner, he keeps talking about "fattening you up." He tells you you're his type; meanwhile, he tells his friends you're his blood type.

The signs of a sinking relationship are unmistakable. Are you really ready to be in this relationship for eternity?

are you ready for eternity?

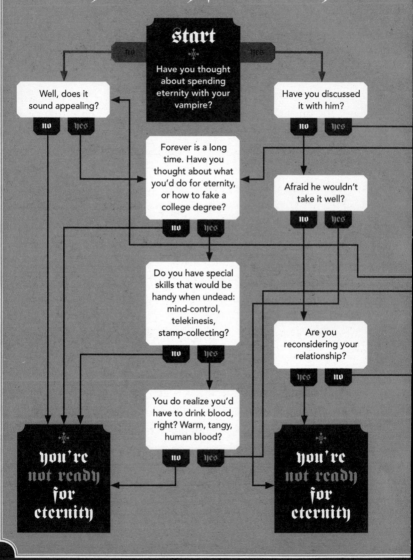

start
+
Have you thought about spending eternity with your vampire?

Well, does it sound appealing?

Have you discussed it with him?

Forever is a long time. Have you thought about what you'd do for eternity, or how to fake a college degree?

Afraid he wouldn't take it well?

Do you have special skills that would be handy when undead: mind-control, telekinesis, stamp-collecting?

Are you reconsidering your relationship?

You do realize you'd have to drink blood, right? Warm, tangy, human blood?

+
you're not ready for eternity

+
you're not ready for eternity

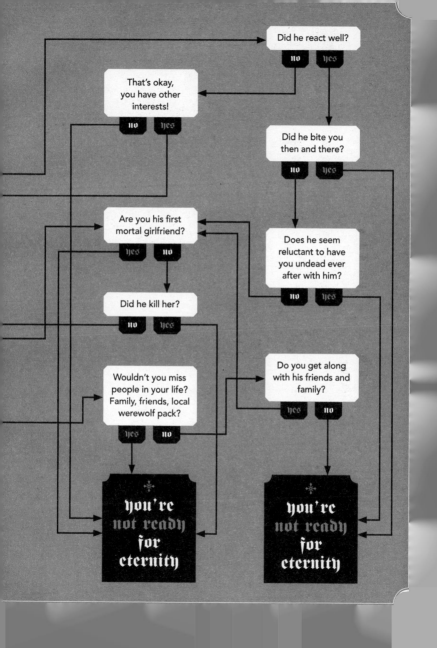

knowing when your relationship has been bled dry

At this point, you're probably ready for an exit interview with your vampire. You humans like to say that all good things must come to an end. Well, news flash: All bad things must come to an end as well. Usually because they're, you know, *bad*.

With vampires, there is no such thing as a toothless breakup. When it's over, you're usually over, too. So you have to tread very carefully if you want to get out of this relationship alive. You might have once had dreams of eternity in your head, but now you are merely hoping to make it to next Thursday. Love hurts, all right. But this kind of hurt is so bad that country music singers don't even have songs about it.

I sort of saw it coming. Nathaniel started acting really strange around me. One day, I tripped and spilled tomato soup all over his white sweater. Instead of grinning and composing an impromptu ode to my endearing human awkwardness, he got pissed and stormed off. (Well, more like floated off, because he moves like a lithe, graceful bobcat, silently stalking his prey across the mossy forest floor. Oh God, I have to stop thinking like this. . . .) He also stopped writing songs for me. When I asked him if I had inspired him lately, he said yes, but looked really uncomfortable as he started to play the piano. After a few moments, I realized that it wasn't an original song at all. He was just playing "Since U Been Gone" really slowly.

Because of Nathaniel's flair for drama, I thought he'd only break up with me at the right moment, so I started to plan my day around organ practice at the local church and the feeding patterns of the neighborhood bird population. I couldn't risk him cornering me while melancholy organ music echoed dolefully around us, or while a flock of doves swooped over our heads. That would be, like, breakup central. But I guess I didn't cover all my bases, because Nathaniel found me at the end of my shift at the library. Before I realized what was happening, he pulled me into the rare books room

and started giving this speech about reaching the final chapter in the story of our love. I pretended not to understand, but then this ugly one-eyed dove landed on the windowsill. (Does this happen in other towns?!) I saw Nathaniel smile slightly as he grasped my hand and fell to his knees. "Oh, Danielle, my life, my love. You are so vulnerable, so innocent—just like that poor, mangled, one-eyed dove." I opened my mouth to protest the comparison but Nathaniel just held a finger to my lips. "No, no. Don't speak, my love. I have blinded you with my glorious beauty and otherworldly perfection. You can no longer see the danger of loving a monster like me. I must leave you forever. And not like the last time, when I left you forever but returned three hours later with an epic poem written in honor of your beauty. Good-bye, darling." He kissed me on the cheek and then swept out of the room, leaving me alone with the staring, ugly bird.

—DANIELLE, 16

I was at the grocery store with my mom picking up cantaloupe when Max texted me: "I think we should see other people/vampires. It's been great. :-)" And I thought vampires were supposed to be classy!

—MEGAN, 16

Of course, the girls in the previous examples got out of it easily. It's impossible for us to get testimonials from the worse-off victims of vampire-related heartbreak, since they are now doornail-style dead. Theirs is a fate you want to avoid—so it's up to you to prepare for whatever breakup scenario your vampire might throw your way.

Trust me, breaking it off isn't as easy as you'd think. Human chicks are just so *emotional*. Hasn't anyone ever told them that blubbering isn't pretty or remotely enticing? Well, someone should! They get so absolutely red in the face and blotchy. And then, if that isn't enough, they get carried away entirely, breaking out the garlic and walking around with a sword! These girls really need help!

—SIMON, 902

I kept telling Emma it was over, but she wouldn't believe me. She kept calling. And texting. And coming by. Finally, I couldn't stand it any longer. I lied and told her I was going to make her eternal. And then, when I made my bite, I finished her (and the relationship) off. I know what you're thinking, and I don't care. The worst thing is, she didn't even taste good, after everything she'd put me through.

—TARQUIN, 73

There's no easy way to end a relationship with a human girl. Love bites. I've found the most effective method is to be a "nice guy." Nothing repels a human girl more than a guy who is too nice.

—MAXIMUS, 765

I opted for the "fade away." I just started seeing her less. And less. And less. One of the great things about being a vampire is our power to outlast humans. Their attention wanders . . . and you can wander to a new town.

—ELIJAH, 313

Penelope was always very melodramatic. I knew it would take a grand gesture to blow her off. So I waited until she was leaving school with all her friends, and I flew up in the sky and spelled out the letters I-A-M-T-H-R-O-U-G-H-W-I-T-H-Y-O-U in red smoke. It was really hot up there, but it was totally worth it to see the look on her face when she realized it was over.

—OREN, 403

affirmations for the end of your relationship

It's so *sweet* that you thought your relationship was going to last. You really imagined that of all the women he's dated over the centuries, *you* would be the one to make it last. Human optimism is just adorable.

It's time to pick up the pieces. When you're not weeping, my dear friend Dr. Thaddeus Phillips, VD, suggests some helpful affirmations for reconnecting with reality.

FROM THE DESK OF DR. THADDEUS PHILLIPS, VD

Gods don't go out with peasants!
Gods don't go out with peasants!

He's better off without me!
He's better off without me!

I never had a chance!
I never had a chance!

The sun might shine again!
The sun might shine again!

I belong with zit-faced teens!
I belong with zit-faced teens!

Of course, you can also resort to the affirmations that Dr. Phillips's ex-wife Dr. Jane Oakes, PhD, suggests.

FROM THE DESK OF DR. JANE OAKES, PhD

No one deserves to be treated like a universal donor — you're special, and you deserve better. I've put together a list of reasons why you made the right decision to kick him to the curb. These are reminders to repeat to yourself when looking in the mirror every morning (because now you can). Repeat one time or repeat ten times. Either way, you'll be over your vamp in no time.

- Pastel is not a dirty word.
- I deserve someone who loves me for me and not just my O-positive blood.
- It is not abnormal to want a date in the daytime.
- Sometimes staring at each other at night under the moonlight gets awkward. And cold.
- It is okay to wear blush. Maybelline, I missed you.
- Yes, it is weird to have three hundred 16th birthdays in a row.
- A cardio workout does not, I repeat, does _not_ consist of giving me a paper cut and seeing how fast I can run to escape.
- It is not worth it to put Fluffy in danger every time my boyfriend comes over.
- It is normal to want my boyfriend to spend time with me instead of strolling in the graveyard every night with his friends.

know you'll never truly be over his godlike posture, his imploring eyes, his pillow-soft lips, his long river of a voice, and/or his rock-solid chest. After all, once you've tasted steak, it's hard to go back to grass. But you need to survive—if only to make the foolish move of falling for a vampire yet again.

Will you buck the general trend of all humanity and learn from your mistakes? Will revenge be yours? Only time—and chapter twelve—will tell.

A NOTE FROM GRETA, A VAMPIRE SLAYER

CALL ME.

choosing
l.o.v.e.

(life over vampire experience)

i think that you and I have grown close over the past eleven chapters. So even though it's not necessarily in my best interests to give away vampire trade secrets, I am going to show you the way to survive a vampire breakup with your self-esteem (and your life) intact.

vlad's vampire breakup survival kit

❀ **HOLY WATER** for the bedside table (in addition, make sure you have a vial for easy toting!).

❀ **MIRRORS,** mirrors everywhere.

❀ **DITTO ON THE GARLIC:** Eat it, hang it, weave it in your hair, and make an aromatic perfume and spray it *everywhere*.

❀ **CROSS YOUR HEART . . .** and your doorway . . . and your bedpost . . . and your window. . . . (Do you think that rosary your grandmother gave you is merely a sweet token of her memory? Think again. She had a little undead drama in her day and knew it would come in handy for your own vampire breakup.)

❀ **A WOODEN STAKE** that's always handy. You can even get ones that fit into a lipstick case!

❀ **A PACKET OF SEEDS** (or Skittles) to sprinkle at your vampire's feet at a moment's notice. Vampires can't stand that.

❀ **BELLS RINGING:** Vampires hate this sound. So get that cowbell off that cow and put it around your waist, dear.

❀ **FRUMPY CLOTHES** with high, high necklines. Like, up to your chin. Or higher.

❀ **WEAPONS:** If it was a *really* bad breakup and your last conversation ended with him swearing eternal vengeance on your very soul, arm yourself with the sharpest, strongest, longest machete, sword, or ax you can find. (Just don't forget to have it blessed!) If everything else fails, you might just have to behead the dude.

are you addicted to dating the undead?

⟨◦⫷▥⟩⟨▥⫸◦⟩

Are all these precautions making you sad? Not because they're inconvenient and imply that he wants you dead, but because you miss him so much? Are you thinking, *The next vampire I date will protect me from this last one. The old model was a fluke.* You mortal sweet thing, you're desperately at risk of becoming a vamp tramp, a fang thang, an immortal portal—that's right, a girl who's addicted to vampire love. Here's a little quiz for you.

1. Are you repulsed by human male habits like leaving the toilet seat up, burping, and breathing?

   a. I can live with it.

   b. I'd rather not deal with the burping.

   c. Ew. Breathing? Gross.

2. Your dream guy:

   a. Is supersmart.

   b. Has a wonderful sense of humor.

   c. Sparkles.

3. What's the best part of having a boyfriend?

   a. Having someone to cut my food lest I sprain my delicate wrists.

   b. Making my friends jealous.

   c. Having someone who cares about me.

4. Your perfect prom date would spend the evening:

   a. Dancing. He loves to bust a move.

   b. Sneering. That's how he rolls.

   c. Moping. He would rather go to a poetry reading.

5. Why did you break up with your last boyfriend?

a. It was getting too serious.

b. He spent too much time with his friends.

c. He got winded when I made him go hiking . . . with me on his back.

6. What's your idea of a perfect date?

a. A romantic walk on the beach.

b. A moonlight visit to a graveyard, where we listen to ravens cry mournfully while we look into the captivating depths of each other's eyes.

c. Dinner and a movie.

7. What's your ideal age difference?

a. I like dating guys my age. We have the most in common.

b. I prefer dating someone two or three years older. Girls mature faster, after all.

c. I only date guys who were born in the nineteenth century. They quote Wordsworth instead of Adam Sandler, and I'm pretty much guaranteed an A in History.

8. Who's your biggest celebrity crush?

a. Zac Efron. I can't resist a guy who sings.

b. Michael Phelps. Athletes are hot.

c. Jonathan Rhys Meyers. I love pale, tortured-looking guys who seem like they might want to kill me.

⇥ Scoring ⇤

TALLY UP YOUR POINTS FOR EACH ANSWER:

1. **a.** 3 **b.** 2 **c.** 0   2. **a.** 3 **b.** 3 **c.** 0   3. **a.** 0 **b.** 1 **c.** 3

4. **a.** 3 **b.** 0 **c.** 2   5. **a.** 3 **b.** 1 **c.** 0   6. **a.** 2 **b.** 0 **c.** 3

7. **a.** 3 **b.** 2 **c.** 0   8. **a.** 1 **b.** 3 **c.** 0

❄ FOR A SCORE OF 0 TO 4

Addicted to dating the undead, you're a vampire vixen. See the rest of this chapter for helpful resources.

❄ FOR A SCORE OF 5 TO 18

You're a sallow siren: You may not be after the captain of the football team, but you still like 'em with a pulse. Keep it up.

❄ FOR A SCORE OF 19 TO 24

A Homo sapiens hottie, you like your boys sexy and smart with a fully operational heart. Congrats! You're poised to live a happy, well-adjusted life.

ten ways to kick your vampire habit

Do you still need help escaping the vampire's seemingly inescapable allure? Well, you could try locking yourself in a small room with no access to the outside world for the rest of your life . . . but that sounds so dreary even to this vampire. Surely, there are other steps you can take.

1 ✳ keep your distance.

Hang out only from sunrise to the hour before sunset to make sure you don't run into him. Better yet, move close to the equator where daylight lasts the longest.

2 ✳ start dating other species.

Remember that kid in second grade you could have sworn was from Mars? Totally not off-limits anymore.

3 ✳ are you hurting? make him hurt.

Grab a voodoo doll and stick some pins and needles in it. Then, throw it in the toaster oven and spend the next day laughing at his weird-looking tan.

4 ✳ starting to blame yourself? blame him instead.

Start a rumor around the graveyard that he's thinking of eating his sister for dinner. Let his clan handle the rest.

5 ✳ start a journal.

Then send it to me for the sequel to this book.

6 ✳ eat. a lot.

Gain back five of those ten pounds you lost when you were too self-conscious to order the garlic knots because he couldn't stand them. Nothing says "I'm over you" better than garlic breath.

7 ✳ throw away any mementos of him, including the first dead flower he gave you, the turtlenecks (with the turtle parts cut off) he bought you, and the subscription to *Vampires Weekly*.

8 ✳ install an electrified grate over your windows.

Yes, some unfortunate hummingbirds may meet a tragic, frizzy end, but it'll be worth it to keep out any peeping Tobiases.

9 ✳ join a vampire lovers anonymous (VLA) support group, and use your dark clothes to help them create a quilt for National I Hate Vampires Day. Reunite with your pal Stevie at the Gap. He's missed you.

10 ✳ buy a pep patch.

(They can be purchased from the VLA.) Rumor has it that one patch a day breathes so much pep back into you that you'll instantly become head cheerleader. It also releases a substance into your bloodstream (I won't specify what) that will make you a little less tasty.

is friendship the answer?

The relationship is dead. The ashes of it are as cold as his sculpted pecs. But you *still* can't move on. He says, "Let's just be friends . . . at least until your mortal life is over." This may sound good, but let's weigh the pros and cons.

pros	cons
You get to feast your eyes on his pearly perfection.	He gets to see you age.
He makes new guys sit up and take notice—you've played in the major leagues!	He makes new guys look puny and pathetic—you'll never play in the major leagues again.
He'll still rescue you from life-threatening situations.	He's the only reason you're in life-threatening situations.
He's available to talk anytime, day or night.	Those bags under your eyes from late-night vampire interactions aren't going to help you land a new guy.
He scares off the serial killers.	He scares off the werewolves.
He can offer a long-term perspective on your problems.	He tells you your problems are insignificant.
He impresses your friends. . . .	. . . until he eats a few of them.

Sensing a theme here? You *can't* be friends with a vampire. Your blood and your history will always get in the way.

vampire alternatives

Breaking up with a vampire is hard to do, and so is dating again when you've just had your heart broken. Before you move on to a new guy, you need to check that impulse to go right for another vampire. As much as you like what a vampire has to offer, it might very well be possible to find a new boyfriend who's not a vampire, but JVE (Just Vampire Enough).

❋ werewolf

They're certainly not as pale as vampires—but it's almost a bonus, because werewolves can go out with you during daylight hours or even accompany you to the beach and come away with tan lines (if they've shaved)! Werewolves can be just as mysterious as vampires—you'll have to keep their secret as closely as you kept your ex-boyfriend's. They can run much faster than you, jump way higher, and are immensely strong—definitely dangerous enough to be JVE. And his loyalty and affection are better than a puppy's!

❋ zombie

Undead? Check. Pale skin? Check. Desire to suck out a part of you that keeps you alive? Check. It sounds like a zombie would have just enough in common with a vampire to keep you interested. All right, so he's decaying a little, and his powers of conversation are sorely lacking (no beautiful sonnets from this guy), but he's still interested in almost nothing but getting close to you. Plus, you have to love a guy who wants a girl for her smarts—or at least for her brains. He might not be able to climb the tree near your window, but he'll surely spend the night right outside, waiting for you to come out.

�֍ elf

Not the little tiny ones with pointy shoes—think tall with long, flowing blond hair and supernaturally good-looking. Elves don't always hang around hobbits. Your new elf BF might be so smitten that he'll give up his immortality to spend the rest of his life with you.

✖ necromancer

Dating a necromancer can be a little creepy—there might be malevolent spirits after him that he'll have to protect you from—and he's always wearing an assortment of bells, which can make it awkward for making out. But you obviously aren't bothered by death, and love a bit of a challenge.

✖ mummy

If you like the strong, silent type and can get over the miles of linen wrapping, a mummy might be JVE for you. Try not to be his first human girlfriend—most mummies come with a nasty curse that kills the first people to unearth their tombs. However, you'll open his eyes (they're in one of the jars near his sarcophagus) if you try to free him from the curse.

✖ ghost

This guy will certainly have supernatural powers and watch over you all night as you sleep—definitely JVE in this way. Make sure to stay away from any poltergeists who might want you dead. Instead, find one with unfinished business, and he'll haunt you as you help him search for the secret keeping him in the physical world.

✖ slayer

If you're out for revenge, this is the next guy you want to date.

It's been so hard to go back to normal life without Marius. I can't help visiting the cemetery where he first told me he was undead, or wandering into the church late at night to sit in a pew and pretend he's next to me. Every time I see something move out of the corner of my eye, I think it's him...and then get sad when I turn and it was just a bird or light reflected on the wall. I haven't gone out much during the day, since there's more of a chance of seeing him if I wait to go out at night. In other words, I need help.

—MARTHA, 19

When Percival broke up with me, I reread all the poems he had written me and noticed that he repeated a lot of phrases. On a whim, I Googled some of the lines and realized that his poems were composed entirely of Celine Dion lyrics. I also noticed that they don't actually make any sense. How could I have swooned at this?

Love can touch us one time.

I drove all night, crept in your room.

Let your heart decide.

O Canada!

Terre de nos aieux?

I'm never dating a real vampire again.

—TERIANN, 15

ou feel like you've been shot in the heart. Everything reminds you of him. Well, open the curtains, curl up on the couch with a cheesy chick flick and a pint of ice cream, and dry your tears! There are plenty of reasons to go on living as a mortal . . . for the next seventy-five to eighty years, anyway.

But what are the reasons to live? I know, you just want to stay buried in your crypt, reminiscing about your dismal relationship. But just think! Now you can enjoy all the things you've been missing: the sun, strolling through gardens, hanging out at the beach, actually eating at mealtimes and not feeling guilty, leaving your pet at home and not worrying that he'll mysteriously disappear, having a big birthday extravaganza without feeling stupid, watching sports other than baseball, kissing a boy without fear that you're undead if he slips, wearing perfume, getting a tan, not hiding scrapes from your boyfriend until they heal, celebrating traditional holidays, cooking vegetables (with garlic!), and so much more.

True, you're not going to live forever, but at least you won't be lying around in a coffin until the Reaper comes for you. So, don't seal yourself up in a mausoleum of pity! Get outside into the sunlight. (No, seriously. Do it. You've probably got a vitamin D deficiency by now.) And try to look on the bright side—life will now be much less gloomy than any of your time spent with your vampire.

You are not alone in this. There are many wonderful organizations and networks that help wayward girls like you.

⟨decorative divider⟩

✠ Slayer hot tips

Did a vampire tell you eternity is not for you? Want a slayer to snatch eternity away from him, too? Call 1-800-555-STAKE-IM.

✠ vampire depression hotline

There's world-weary, and then there is despair. If you think he's *really* down and not just brooding to be sexy, call the Vampire Depression Hotline (listed in your local phone book). It's not like he can kill himself, but he *can* kill your whole town.

✠ vampires anonymous

Don't get excited. This is not a support group *for* vampires, where you can pick up a sexy Thaddeus or Frederick of your very own. This is a twelve-step program for hapless humans who are addicted to dating vampires. (At local churches everywhere.)

⟨decorative divider⟩

N̲ow, dear human reader, I am afraid it is time for Vlad to say *au revoir*. I hope I have been able to illuminate the pleasures and perils of dating vampires in a way that you will take to heart, if not to mind.

As for me—I must presently leave you. I have to go get ready for a date with a girl not unlike yourself. The crucial difference? She doesn't like to read.

Poor, poor girl. A book like this would have helped her so very much.